Honey House

A KC Carmichael Novel

Laura Harner

Copyright © 2011 by Laura Harner

Cover photography purchased from 123RF Stock Photography

Cover Art by Laura Harner

Edited by Jae Ashley

All rights reserved.

Published in the United States by Hot Corner Press

ISBN: 978-1-937252-79-3

Second Edition

Dedication

To Virgie and Diane, for always believing in me. Words are not enough.

Acknowledgement of Trademarks

Chapter One

My name is Katherine Carmichael and I don't do breakfast. Fact was, I might just have rolled in for the night by the time most people are up and heading to work. The idea of owning a bed and breakfast was ridiculous. Of course, since I didn't own anything, the whole idea was even more absurd. There had to be a catch. I looked at the note once more, as if I hadn't already memorized it.

> *KC,*
>
> *My attorney has taken care of the legalities, and I have taken care of the rest. The Honey House is waiting for you. It's time you know what you really are.*
>
> *Good luck, dear.*

There was a hastily added postscript: *P.S. Don't try to change the name. The House won't like it.*

I folded the note and slipped it into the side pocket of my purse, then climbed out of the limousine. The door of the long stretch barely closed before the machine glided smoothly away leaving me standing outside the Honey House Bed and Breakfast. I took the keys and slowly walked up the pathway, through a sandstone and wood beam archway, and across a wide porch. I looked over my shoulder as I slipped the key into the lock, half-expecting to be arrested for breaking and entering. The knob turned easily, and I walked through the doorway into a stunning foyer worthy of Southwest Showplaces magazine. Maybe the circumstances were leaving me feeling a little fanciful, but I could swear I felt the house settle around me. That was disturbing.

I appreciated the effect. Setting atmosphere is the first step in running a successful con. I should know... I've been running cons for years. Apparently, the old lady who wrote the note was running a doozy of a scam, because she'd gone to a lot of trouble to set this whole thing up. Whatever this whole thing was.

"Hello," I called out to the empty house.

"Over here," whispered a voice from deep in the shadows.

I grinned. Yep, a most excellent con. Joanne, the woman behind this particular show, was a former client. I'd thought she'd been one of the happy ones. I'd met her a few months ago in the middle of my most recent gig, working on a cruise ship as a fortuneteller. Okay, I suppose it's technically not a con, because officially, I'm part of the onboard entertainment. I receive a salary, meals, and a miniscule cabin as compensation for my work. My customers are free to tip me, and that turns a low paying job into a very good living. I travel back and forth to Mexico on the three to five day cruises that depart from Long Beach.

When I'd stepped off the ship this morning, Joanne's 'lawyer' had been waiting for me. He'd told me I'd inherited a bed and breakfast in Juniper Springs, a small community outside Sedona, Arizona. That had nearly sent me into a fit of giggles. Everyone knew Juniper Springs was as genuine as professional wrestling.

"The New Age Mecca?" I'd choked out, my voice full of sarcasm.

The painfully thin young lawyer had stiffened. "Many people claim to have experienced spiritual or metaphysical events, however, I assure you I have never personally witnessed anything unusual."

He was good. I could almost believe he was straight out of law school, instead of a fellow con artist. Of course, he wasn't as good as I was, but I'd played along.

"Okay, lawyer-boy, what's the plan?"

"The limousine is waiting to take us to the airport," he'd said.

I'd looped my arm through his. "Let's go. I'm up for an adventure."

That had been hours, one private plane, and two limo rides ago. Now I was about to discover what this was all about. I suspected Joanne wanted me to work for her at the B and B. The Honey House was perfectly located in the heart of the paranormal tourism country; it would be a boon to have a pet psychic on staff. She must have just recently bought the place, because although it was architecturally stunning, it looked and felt unused. Based on the size of the show she was putting on to lure me here, the job must be worth a lot of money. I was impressed.

"In here," the voice whispered again, apparently impatient at my hesitation.

This was really cool and more than a little creepy. I passed through the entryway and down two steps into an open seating area, with cream-colored plastered walls and a high, open beam ceiling. Large terra cotta tiles lined the floor, interspersed every few feet with small, brightly colored ceramic tiles that brought the flavor of Mexico into the spacious room. I scanned the area looking for Joanne.

I found her in front of the massive stone fireplace, lying face down in a pool of blood.

"Joanne!" Completely forgetting this was all part of the act, I raced to the crumpled body on the floor. Despite my thudding heart and nearly overwhelming instinct to run, I felt for a pulse and my fingers came away from her neck sticky with congealed blood.

Certain details were like a stake to my heart. Body, bloody knife, ex-convict. Then I remembered this was all supposed to be a con.

Suddenly, this wasn't very funny. I spun around, looking for the source of the voice that had lured me in here. The room appeared empty. The front door opened then closed with sharp click of the latch. Heavy footfalls came slowly toward me. I only had seconds before I would be discovered alone with a dead body and blood on my hands. Shit!

"Miss Carmichael?" a man's voice boomed out.

Looking down at the body, I felt uncertain as hell. This was too real to be a con. I could smell the coppery odor of the blood. I was way out of my league.

A tall figure in a uniform stepped from the shadows of the entryway. A cop. Double shit.

"There you are. I promised Malcolm I would walk through the building when you got here to make sure everything was okay, but I was delayed. Sorry 'bout that. Name's MacQuinnlan." His deep, gravelly voice spoke of whisky or smoke, or both.

"I didn't—"

I trailed off, not wanting to admit to anything in front of a cop, not even my innocence.

He took off his cowboy hat and looked at me strangely. His hair was sun-streaked brown and his eyes were some kind of weird light color. His crisp khaki uniform shirt topped comfortably faded blue jeans, and he wore the obligatory cowboy boots of the area. Boy, did he take up a lot of space in the room. More space than even his six-foot, plus-something frame demanded. He wasn't that much older than my twenty-four years, but something in those weird eyes felt ancient. They were cop eyes.

Which brought me back to Joanna's dead body. I looked down, nauseated at the sight and smell of all the blood. Would he believe I didn't have anything to do with the body if I threw up on the evidence? Nah, probably not. On the other hand, he must not be the brightest bulb in the box if he was stuck out here in the sticks. He hadn't even noticed the dead body between us on the floor. Yeah, not too bright.

"Look, Officer—"

"It's Sheriff," he interrupted.

"Okay, Sheriff. I know what this might look like," I swept my hand out, gesturing to Joanne without looking at her, "but I swear I didn't do anything."

He reached me in two giant strides and took my outstretched arm. "I don't know what the hell you're talking about, but let's go. I don't have all night. I'll walk through each room, make sure none of the local kids or anyone else snuck in here while the place's been vacant."

I looked down in horror to see if he'd actually stepped on Joanne's body or just in the blood. There was nothing there.

****

We ended the tour of the facility in the owner's unit on the southeast corner of the building. I stayed quiet, completely freaked out by the disappearing dead body in the great room. MacQuinnlan paid no attention to me other than to tell me to lift the dust cloths and look under the beds. He raced us through every room, quickly examining each door, window, and closet.

I tried to take it all in, really I did. The entire place was fantastic, with authentic eighteen-inch thick adobe walls, stone fireplaces, and either peeled-log or open beam ceilings. There were thirteen guest suites, a giant kitchen, a dining room, great room, plus a library. The owner's apartment consisted of two floors, four rooms, and was as beautifully appointed as any of the luxurious suites I'd just visited.

It was all too much. Something very strange was happening, and I didn't trust the sheriff to tell me anything. Something about him was off. When he'd turned his back to me the first time, I'd been surprised to see his hair wasn't short, as I'd originally thought. Masses of golden brown waves spilled from an elastic ponytail holder to end several inches below his massive shoulders.

I narrowed my eyes, thinking. What was real? What wasn't? I'd never seen a longhaired cop before. He was dressed unconventionally for a cop, too. Seriously...jeans and cowboy boots? It occurred to me that I'd been very stupid to take his word that he was the sheriff. When had I turned into such a chump? I'd followed the man through an empty house without even a momentary consideration of the possible consequences of being alone in a strange place with a likely criminal. Even if he was posing as a sheriff.

No doubt about it...I was off my game. I turned slowly to look at him, wondering for the umpteenth time what in the hell was going on. It was time to bring things to a head.

"Okay, look. I know this is some kind of scam. You and lawyer-boy...you're both in on this. Just actors, right? Joanne's not really dead, she wants me to come work for her, doesn't she? That's what this is all about, isn't it?" I asked.

MacQuinnlan looked at me long and hard. Up this close and personal, I could see the unusual color of his eyes. They were a rich golden-honey with flecks of brown and green. And they were looking at me from a mask of tightly-controlled anger.

"Lawyer-boy? You mean Malcolm? You're some smart ass, aren't you?" Without waiting for an answer to what I figured was probably a rhetorical question, the sheriff continued. "Joanne is gone and she was a friend of mine," MacQuinnlan gritted out through a tightly clenched jaw.

"I checked you out when Joanne left you this place. I know about your parents and I know you went to juvenile detention when they went to prison. I know you like to run little scams, and you don't have the balls to run the big ones. I know about your little psychic fortune-telling act.

"Near as I can tell, Joanne only met you once, when she was on that cruise to Mexico, so I don't understand how she knew enough about you to decide. However, if Joanne says you belong in the House, then she had her reasons. I don't have to understand it, and I don't have to like it. Good evening, Miss Carmichael," MacQuinnlan said, jamming his hat on his head as he turned on his heel and left. I jumped when I heard the front door slam.

With a little bit of an 'I don't give a shit' flourish, I grabbed an afghan from the back of a chair and wrapped it tightly around my shoulders. I was still dressed in my casual end-of-cruise capris and tee and starting to get damn cold. Wasn't it always supposed to be hot in Arizona?

I thought about everything that had happened since law— Malcolm talked me into a plane ride earlier. Nothing had changed. I still believed this was some kind of scam. The body and blood were gruesome, but they hadn't been real. They couldn't have been. The crew had pulled out all the stops, and the whole B and B angle was interesting. Weighing the options of staying to hear the pitch or heading back to Long Beach, I decided enough was enough. As con games went, this one was spectacular, but I wasn't into that scene anymore.

Once I decided not to stick around for the next act of this bizarre little play, I began to plan. A cab to take me to Sedona and then a shuttle from there to the Phoenix airport. It would be a long night of travel, but at least I would be home by morning. Home. What a laugh.

A sense of urgency to escape washed over me. I faked looking cool as I race-walked through the empty house toward the front door. Not because I was scared, just because it made me feel better.

I turned the corner from the great room to the entryway and slammed to a stop, staring at the woman blocking the door.

"Hello, KC."

"Joanne?" I stammered, confused by her appearance. I looked around for the projector. The figure in front of me was the image of Joanne, only set to a seventy percent transparency. Apparently, I was going to get to see the next act of the play. Like it or not.

I reminded myself she wasn't real, then pushed my hand through the illusion and reached for the doorknob.

It all happened rapid fire: the smell of sulfur, a crack of electricity, me flying through the air. I landed against the wall, and my head hit hard enough to make me see stars.

Chapter Two

"You're pale as a ghost, dear."

"Funny, Joanne," I said, wandering around the room looking for a projector.

"Yes, I thought so," the transparent figure agreed, smiling rather smugly. "KC, stop. You know there aren't any smoke and mirrors involved. I'm really a ghost and the Honey House is yours. Now, please sit down. I have very little time and you must have a lot of questions."

"Very little time? Not that I'm admitting you're a ghost, but say you were…where exactly would you need to be?"

"Why Rome, of course. I've always wanted to visit. There's a couple in town who are leaving for the airport in a few minutes, and I want to catch a ride. I'll start by telling you what I think you need to know, and if there's time, you can ask questions at the end."

*

Now, in the pale light of the morning, I sat alone in the dining room with my third cup of coffee, thinking over the events of the previous night. It had taken quite a while to convince me, and I still wasn't sure I believed all of it, but what the hell? You had to believe in something. It seemed Joanne really was dead, and as long as I didn't mind an occasional ghostly visit, the Honey House was indeed mine.

I looked around appreciatively. The décor was faultlessly southwestern, with stained glass accents and plants everywhere. The dark wooden tables and ladder-back chairs contrasted beautifully with the tile floors and were spaced to offer a modicum of privacy. I counted thirteen tables, same as the number of guest suites. Good thing I'm not superstitious.

The dining room faced west, so it was still a little dim, but the front windows were large and the view of red rock spires against the morning sky was spectacular. I couldn't wait to explore outside.

The first order of business, once sufficient quantities of caffeine were consumed, was to find out who'd been watering the plants since Joanne had died. Maybe that same person could tell me more about the bed and breakfast. Ghostly Joanne was strangely reticent on discussing the business. In fact, her sole focus seemed to be on convincing me that the house and I belonged to each other, and how important it was that I stay to at least try it out.

Strange as it seemed in the cool light of morning, I hadn't wanted to run out of the house screaming at the sight of Joanne's…ghost…spirit…whatever you wanted to call her. I hadn't been scared once Joanne appeared and started talking to me. I wonder why that was? Anyway, what's the old adage? In for a penny, in for a pound. There was no way I would leave now. Not without knowing the secrets of the mysterious Honey House.

The front door opened and the approaching footsteps echoed through the quiet morning, eerily reminiscent of the previous evening. Once again, it was the sheriff. With an exaggerated sigh, he threw a stack of newspapers on the table near me. Without a word, he stalked straight into the kitchen. When he returned a minute later, it was with a mug of coffee and a deep scowl.

"You're going to need Botox if you don't stop frowning like that," I said, a bit flippantly. "How did you get in here, anyway? Don't you knock?"

"Funny, Miss Carmichael." He grabbed the sports section and took it to a table near the large front window. He hooked a foot around a chair, pulled it back, and sat.

I stared holes in him, but he never even looked up. His arrogant assumption that he was welcome to drop in whenever he chose was more than my inner bitch could take at this hour of the morning.

"Excuse me, Sheriff; I don't remember telling you to make yourself at home. Now how the hell did you get in here?"

"Told you," he mumbled, not looking up. "Door was unlocked. Call me Quinn." He turned the page.

Grrr…this was not going well. *God, I hate mornings.*

Quinn looked up, as if finally realizing I was staring at him.

"Where's the bagels?" he asked.

My jaw dropped. "Bagels? You stroll in here at the crack of dawn, make yourself at home, and expect bagels?" I knew my voice was rising dangerously, but seriously, this was too much. "Tell me how you got in. If you have a key, I want it back. Now."

Quinn pushed his chair back from the table and rocked onto the rear legs. He stared at me speculatively for a long moment, with those strange amber eyes. He began explaining, each word enunciated to within an inch of its life.

"First, it's hardly the crack of dawn. When I did come by at the crack of dawn, the door wasn't opened yet, even though the dining room opens at six. Second, your coffee tastes like shit and your hospitality isn't much better. Third—"

The front door opened and a voice called out, "Hello. Anybody home?"

"In here," Quinn and I shouted together, then turned and glared at each other. *What the hell?*

"Hi, I know it's too early for check in, but I'm really hoping you have a room I can rent for a week. Every room in Sedona is booked for spring break, and I'm on deadline. My name's Jason. Jason Brill. With the Arizona Chronicle." His voice rose at the end like a question, but he continued, rapid fire. "I'm up here doing a story on the sweat lodge deaths. Glad to find you here, Sheriff. It will save me a trip to the station. Do you think I could get a cup of that coffee?" Jason finally wound down to wait for an answer.

"I wouldn't recommend it," said Quinn. "It tastes like shit."

Ignoring Quinn, I turned to the reporter. "Look, Mr. Brill," I began, but he interrupted.

"Jason," he repeated firmly, "and you are—"

"Katherine Carmichael, but please, call me KC. I'm sorry, but I just found out about—"

The door to the kitchen swung open behind me, and a tall, sultry-looking Latina woman pushed her way through with a tray of bagels and condiments in one hand and a carafe of coffee in the other.

This place was Grand Central Station, and I didn't have a ticket.

"Morning, Quinn," she said in a rich contralto.

"Buenos días, Gabrielle," Quinn answered, smiling at the woman.

I had a brief moment to wonder what it might be like to have the force of that smile turned in my direction. *Wow.* With a shake of my head at the absurdity of that random thought, I tried to catch up to what was happening around me.

Gabrielle settled the serving tray onto a buffet, turned to the reporter, and smiled. "Of course we have a room for you. Jason, was it? I'm afraid we've been closed due to a recent change in ownership, so bear with us. You just sit and enjoy your coffee and talk to Quinn. KC and I will get your room ready."

She looped her arm through mine. "Come with me," she stage whispered. As we left the room, she said over her shoulder, "Get a fresh cup of coffee, Quinn, I made a new pot."

With the sinking sensation that I was falling through a rabbit hole, I followed Gabrielle, taking two steps for everyone one of her long strides. She loped to the front desk and grabbed a stack of fresh linens and towels, from the antique armoire behind the bar that served as a counter. Without a word she led the way to a suite of rooms on the first floor, next to the library. As soon as we were inside and the door was closed she let loose with bubbling laughter. It was a rich, deep laugh, and I smiled automatically in response.

Shaking my head, I started. "Want to tell me who you are and exactly what is going on around here?"

"Sorry," she gasped. "The expression on your face was priceless." She dabbed at the tears gathering in the corners of her eyes.

"Wait a minute. You mean this *is* all a hoax?" I hissed indignantly.

"No, no, not at all. I'm sorry. Let me start over. I'm Gabrielle Martinez. You can call me Gabi, if you like. I answer to either. I helped Joanne manage the place. I just assumed we'd open for business, now that you're here. The House doesn't like to be closed."

"The House doesn't like to be closed? What the hell does that mean? And where did you come from this morning? I didn't hear you come in." This laughing woman, so near my own age intrigued me. I was sure she could tell me what was going on around here.

"Didn't Joanne explain? The Honey House has a mind of its own. Look, I know this is all very new to you, but you're going to have to trust me on this. No one comes in the House that isn't supposed to. Once someone comes through that door and asks for a room, we give it to him.

"Now help me make the bed, and I'll tell you what I can." Gabrielle put the stack of fresh linens on the chair and took the fitted sheet first. With a snap of her wrists, she billowed the sheet over the mattress and I quickly moved to the other side of the bed and caught the edge. We worked companionably while she talked.

"I came in through the kitchen door. You probably didn't hear me when I came in because you had your hands full with Quinn. I wasn't sure how much Joanne told you about our arrangement..."

Fifteen minutes later, we were back in the dining room, and I was more confused than ever. I'm not usually so slow on the uptake, but the things Gabi spoke of sounded like real haunted house stuff. Well, I guess I already knew that, since I'd seen Joanne, but still... No one ever showed up unless we had a room for them, the doors unlocked and locked themselves when the House wanted to be open. Furniture rearranged itself? *Sheesh*.

The doorbell rang before I got back to my coffee and a man in brown was waiting with a hand truck full of boxes.

"Where should I put this?" he asked.

I checked the paperwork and was surprised to see it was from the cruise line. A note from the bursar included my last paycheck and a thank you. I was officially unemployed. Or rather, self-employed. How in the hell had that happened since yesterday?

I led the way to the owner's apartment and directed him to leave the stack of boxes just inside the door. Then we retraced our steps to the front of the building where he politely refused a tip. He gave a little wave as he wheeled his hand truck into the back of his truck, then climbed in and drove away. When I closed the door it was with the sensation that I had somehow closed the door on another chapter of my life.

No one looked up when I paused in the doorway of the dining room. Gabi was sitting at one of the small tables drinking coffee with Quinn. Jason and his cup were both absent, so I assumed he had taken his coffee to his room. It seemed like a good opportunity to be alone. I was still completely in the dark about why a woman I'd met briefly on a five-day cruise would bequeath me her business. Joanne-the-ghost had said the House selected me. When I'd asked Gabi, she'd backed Joanne, and said I was the "House choice". It made me feel like a salad dressing. Funny woman, that Gabi.

Moving slowly through the empty hallway, past the closed doors of the vacant guestrooms, all the way to the back of the house, I thought about the whole *woowoo* aspect of the situation. Three years ago, I'd have scoffed at anyone who'd told me psychics were real. I'd been a "fortune teller" for a year by that time, and yes, it was an act. It was an act, because everything I knew about being a psychic came from the *Paranormal for Idiots* guidebook.

Ask a lot of questions and then tell the clients what they want to hear.

One day I'd been holding an old man's hand, preparing to tell his fortune. I'd started asking questions, gently probing about his circumstances, just as I always did. Then I'd felt something I'd never experienced before. It was as if some great darkness washed over me, leaving me cold and clammy. There was a horrible taste in my mouth and I fought against my gag reflex. The man was sick. I couldn't explain how I knew, but I did. He didn't.

His wife was waiting when he'd come out. He'd looked a little sheepish and told her nothing much had happened. I'd interrupted and told her to take him to the doctor as soon as possible, and everything would be all right. Six months later, I'd received a note of thanks and a check for two thousand dollars. Apparently, on a full physical, his doctor had discovered a previously undiagnosed medical condition, and the early intervention saved his life.

Soon other things had started to come to me during these sessions. Not every time, but enough to make me wonder. I'd started buying more books and reading up on psychic ability and my popularity on the cruises increased exponentially. I still wasn't completely ready to call myself a psychic, but it was getting harder to argue against it.

A shiver passed through me and pulled me back to the present. I rubbed my arms against the chill of the morning. I needed warmer clothes if I was going to stay in Juniper Springs. *Stay?* The thought surprised me. It seemed as though I *would* be staying, at least for a while. I made a mental list: clothes, food, and a better understanding of the House rules.

First order of business, go back and find Gabrielle to get answers to my questions. I looked down at my sleep-rumpled capris and ran a hand through my tangled black hair. Okay, maybe the first order of business was a shower and clean clothes, but then I would find Gabrielle.

Once inside, I leaned against the door and sighed deeply. Although I'd taken a brief look around last night, my thoughts had been scattered…certainly not focused on the layout of my new apartment. A secret thrill ran through me at those words. *My new apartment.* I'd never owned anything before. Okay, sure I owned a laptop, an iPod, things like that, but nothing solid. Nothing I wouldn't be willing to leave behind. It had been one of my foster parent's first lessons. Never leave them enough rope to hang you. I'd learned early to travel light.

It was why the gig on the ship had been so perfect. Most of my co-workers went on three or four cruises a month, returning to their own homes and families in between. I'd taken every cruise I could get, often leaving one ship and boarding the other in the same morning. I'd hated when the cruises overlapped and I was forced to miss one. I would hole up in the employee bunkroom and wait for the next ship to be readied. Fortunately, even in winter the cruise line offered a near-continuous schedule.

My new place had a bedroom, with a king-sized bed, a study, a living room, and combination eating and cooking area. It was as well-appointed as the finest of the first class cabins, only roomier. The bedroom and study shared a large, private balcony on the second floor. The view was spectacular, with soaring red rock formations layered against a sky so blue it made my throat tight.

This could be bad. I could begin to care for this place, which would break the second rule my parents taught me. Don't get attached; you can't lose what you don't love.

Steeling my heart, I realized I needed to treat this like any other gig. It still could be a scam. Everyone's story was consistent, every piece looked real, but great cons always started that way. I'd worked hard at staying out of the cheat, but if I was somehow back in the middle of it, then I would play the game.

Chapter Three

It had been two busy weeks since I first came to the Honey House. It turned out Gabi only worked part-time. It was up to me to make the breakfast part of the Bed and Breakfast. I'd learned to make better coffee, and breakfast consisted of bagels, fruit, and yogurt delivered by the local grocers. That was gourmet by my standards.

The sheriff continued to show up for breakfast every morning, complaining because the House apparently had made a concession to my dislike of early mornings by opening its doors an hour later than it previously had. He rarely spoke and never paid, but he had become part of my morning routine. I'd say it was comforting, but that would be a lie. Quinn just wasn't a comfortable person to be around.

On the bright side, Jason, the good-looking reporter from Phoenix had returned today. He was excited because the newspaper had decided to run his story on the sweat lodges as a part of a series on the paranormal tourism industry. Juniper Springs had long been a hot spot for paranormal groupies. Jason had been a bit evasive when I'd asked if his article was an exposé or a tourism feature.

Interest in the small community had really heated up in the past year, once pictures had shown up on the Internet that purported to be of a real werewolf at a local ranch. Now both Juniper Springs and her much larger neighbor Sedona had thousands of annual visitors seeking to purchase crystals, have their aura's read, or even take jeep rides into the desert in order to sit in spiritual vortexes. Apparently, one paranormal craze fed all the others. So far, the Honey House wasn't on any paranormal radar, but it would certainly fit right in there.

If seeing Jason again was on the upside, there was definitely a downside to the day, as well. I was looking forward to the evening about as much as a trip to the dentist.

Gabi stood in the doorway to my bedroom and didn't bother to hide her smile when I pouted as I slipped on my heels.

"Come on, KC, it's just a small dinner party," Gabi coaxed. "This will be fun. You've been working too hard since you arrived. This way you get to meet the other locals on your own turf. Let me look at you," she said, and cocked her head to the side. "Ah, black and blue. This is what you are wearing to a party?" Her soft accent lilted and soothed the insult.

"What's wrong with what I'm wearing?" I asked, feeling put out.

"Actually, nothing. It's just a bit more business-like than I expected." She smoothed her hands over my waist and across my hips. "Chica, you have the best figure in town. Not all the women will be happy, so maybe the muted colors are a good choice for tonight. Come, let me put your hair up for you."

We stood together, Gabrielle behind me, and looked in the mirror. With a few twists and the help of a large clip, Gabrielle created a casual upsweep of hair that left plenty of lose strands curling around my face and neck. She planted a kiss on my cheek. "KC, I take it all back. The blue is a perfect complement to your eyes. You look lovely. Now let's go down and get this party started!"

Gabrielle had arranged the catered event and seating was under the twinkle lights on the courtyard patio. All I had to do was show up and be sociable. Not exactly my best skill. Gabrielle took it upon herself to introduce me to everyone, and she kept one arm looped through mine for comfort.

Two men casually walked toward us, smiling. "KC," Gabrielle said, "let me introduce you to Owen and Gregory, owners of the G&O. It's the organic grocery where all the breakfast supplies come from."

"KC," the one called Owen said, offering his hand with a grin. Gregory pushed his hand aside and swept me into a bone-crunching hug that lifted me off my feet.

"Welcome, girl! It's high time we got to meet you. You are *gorgeous*," he said. "Let me see." He twirled me around, looking admiringly at the long expanse of bare leg showing below my short black skirt. "Oh very nice, très chic. I see you'll give our Susan a run for her money."

Then he leaned in conspiratorially, and stage-whispered, "Are those breasts real?"

I laughed, as Owen blushed and tried to shush the outrageous Gregory. These were two seriously fine-looking men. Owen was tall, with the solid build of a lumberjack, glossy brown hair, and smoky gray eyes a lover could get lost in for hours. Gregory was slightly shorter and not quite as broad across the chest. His blue eyes, darker than my own, danced with merriment. I took no offense to the senseless flirtation. In fact, I loved it! Of course, I needed to give a little dish back.

I sighed theatrically and rolled my eyes to glance over at Gabi. "Why, oh why, are all the good-looking men either already taken or gay?"

Gregory's eyes went wide just for a second, before Owen's laughter rang out. "Welcome, KC." Owen smiled, extending his hand again. "I see Susan may not be the only one you challenge," he said, looking at his partner's grinning face.

I was definitely going to enjoy getting to know these two beautiful men. The night was looking up. I'd missed the admiring looks I used to get on the cruises, and even though Gregory and Owen were clearly a couple, they would spare me some appreciative glances. I was pretty sure I'd get one from Jason, too.

As Gabrielle had observed, the clingy, deep-blue sweater was the perfect shade to highlight my eyes, which I thought were my best feature. As Gregory pointed out, though, I did have nice breasts. Most men commented on my breasts before they ever said anything about my eyes, so it could be that I was wrong about my best feature.

I looked around the patio and noticed Quinn entering with a willowy blonde on his arm. I only had a moment to wonder if she was his date before Gabrielle swept me away from the safety of my new friends to introduce me to the latest arrivals.

"How do you do? I'm Katherine Carmichael, please call me KC." I offered a hand. The woman looked at it just long enough to be rude. Just as I was dropping mine, she languidly raised her own, forcing me to make a second effort to take her hand.

"My name is Susan. Please don't shorten it. I find nicknames rather juvenile. Perhaps you should visit my store, Elegant Rocks. I'm sure I could find you some suitable pieces," she drawled, eyeing my bare throat and ear lobes.

Hey, if I didn't own it, people couldn't steal it. That was my motto. She was deliberate in her snottiness, but I'd been treated like the help before. I knew her type and she didn't intimidate me. I took a long look at her hand clutching Quinn's arm, her perfectly painted red nails digging into his golden tanned forearm. I smiled. This was going to be like stealing candy from a baby.

I took a step forward, and she flinched slightly, before pulling away, as though she feared I might strike her. I squirmed between her and Quinn, placed both of my hands on his forearm, and turned the two of us away from her. With a flutter of lashes to support the innocence of my statement, I looked up and said, "Poor

Quinn, I'm sure she didn't mean it about your nickname." Then I dragged him to the fire pit, well out of Susan's reach.

He was shaking when I let loose of his arm, and I glanced up expecting to see fury all over his face. Instead, he was struggling to keep his face composed; it was laughter making those big shoulders shake. With his back to Susan, he grinned at me. It was the first genuine show of any emotion other than supreme irritation he'd aimed my way.

"Okay, round one to you, Miss Carmichael. I'd watch my back if I were you, though. Susan isn't known for her gentleness around other women; around other *things,* yes, around other women, not so much," he added with a throaty growl.

"Oh really? What types of other things?" I asked sweetly, as if I cared. Why had I just stuck my nose in their business? I didn't care if he wanted to boff some woman old enough to be his…okay, maybe not his mother, but surely, she was old enough to be his older sister. *Much* older sister. It was just Susan's catty attitude that got to me. I didn't even like the muscle-bound sheriff. Although looking at him in his dark gray slacks, and form-fitting jade sweater, I had to admit, he did clean up well.

"Oh, you know," he said, lowering his head conspiratorially. "The things that make a man feel—"

"Excuse me, Sheriff, I see my date," I said and walked to Jason, leaving Quinn hunched over, whispering to where my ear had been an instant before. He looked startled that I'd walked away, but I didn't want to hear his sexual innuendo. I'm no prude, far from it. However, Sheriff Quinn was not my idea of safe sex. Besides a condom, safe sex included a man who didn't try to intimidate me every time I turned around and a man who could be depended on to leave when the time was right.

I certainly didn't need a man for my happily ever after. If I ever decided to settle down—a situation I highly doubted—but if I did? The man would be my partner and my equal in every sense.

The rest of the evening passed uneventfully. I met a banker, several artists, a chef, a spa owner, and the head of the Chamber of Commerce. There was only a small moment of awkwardness when Gabrielle's husband Raymond asked Jason about the story he was investigating. No one seemed particularly thrilled that it might be turning into an exposé on several of the local paranormal businesses.

Jason was clearly uncomfortable revealing too many details, but everyone already knew he was investigating the sweat lodge deaths. No one minded if Ted Sparks, the self-proclaimed new age guru, went down for what he'd done. In fact, everyone here seemed to think he was guilty of killing the four people who died after paying him thousands of dollars for a "spiritual cleansing." The real problem was no one was sure what other businesses Jason was targeting.

The conversation dwindled, then into the relative silence that sometimes occurs in a crowd, Quinn said,

"Miss Carmichael has a bit of her own experience with paranormal business, isn't that right?"

"KC," Gregory laughed, "you've been holding out on me. What's your specialty? Crystals? Vortex tours?"

It pissed me off that Quinn would bring up my past in such a public way. Was he going to expose all my secrets? My parents? Jail? *Shit.*

I just smiled, so Quinn continued, "Miss Carmichael is a rather famous psychic. Our very own fortune teller." He turned that amber gaze on me, his look mocking, and quirked an eyebrow. He was angry that I'd walked away from him earlier. This, his look said, was his revenge.

Susan, apparently eager to twist the knife, said, "Oh please, let's have a demonstration of your…talents."

"Oh, I don't think so," I said, trying to keep my voice casual. "I think my hands are full enough with running the Honey House. I put away my Tarot cards and crystal ball," I added lightly.

Gabrielle asked who wanted dessert, and the conversation moved on. I risked a glance at Quinn, wanting to incinerate him on the spot. He was looking at me, too. I raised my glass in a mocking salute, and he returned the gesture. I'd embarrassed him earlier, and his retaliation was swift. We both knew he could have told more, but he'd stopped. He was holding back ammunition for future skirmishes. Round one was over, and we'd both drawn blood.

****

Jason and I turned to each other in the quiet after the last of the dinner guests had left. He was a handsome man, with short auburn hair, warm brown eyes, and a great smile. It was clear he wanted me, but I wasn't sure the feeling was mutual. Living at the Honey House complicated the situation. He could invite me to his room, which would make it seem very much as if I was agreeing to sex. We could go to the great room, which would make it seem as though I was saying no to anything too personal. Or, we could go to my place, which was a definite maybe.

He stepped forward and placed his hands on my waist, and very slowly lowered his mouth to mine. His kiss was gentle and warm, like everything about him. "I don't want this evening to end yet, KC," he whispered.

"Come to my place," I whispered back. "We can have a nightcap and talk." I knew I was sending mixed messages, but damned if I wasn't receiving mixed messages from my own body.

We held hands, and the warm flesh against flesh was nice in the increasing chill of the night air. When we entered my apartment, Jason turned and pressed me against the door. He placed one hand on either side of my head. When I didn't stop him, he slowly lowered his mouth to cover mine. Then gentle Jason suddenly wasn't quite so gentle anymore. He kissed me long and hard, and pressed something equally hard against my stomach.

I wrapped my arms around his neck and pulled him closer, moaning softly into his mouth. His kisses were warm and wet, and it had been a long time since someone had wanted me like this. Jason slid his hands underneath my sweater, and caressed my back, before slowly sliding to the front and palming my breasts through my bra, his thumbs rubbing against my nipples.

Pulling back from the kiss, he whispered against my neck, "I want you, KC."

His words brought a touch of reality back to me. This was supposed to be my *maybe* place, and I had walked in and telegraphed yes…yes…yes. I tried to pull further back, but I was stuck between a hard door at my back and a hard Jason at my front nuzzling my neck.

"Jason, wait. Please, let's slow down for a minute, okay? Let me get us that drink I promised." I pushed at his shoulders to add emphasis.

With a shaky breath, Jason released me. I led him to the couch and went to the small kitchen. "Macallan or Irish Cream?" I asked. A man's drink said a lot about him.

"Irish Cream, I don't even know what Macallan is," he laughed.

I laughed too, but knew that was one strike against him. I'd gotten used to drinking top shelf on the cruises, and there was no finer single malt whisky, in my book. While I poured the drinks, Jason busied himself with something on my coffee table.

When I joined him on the couch, I was dismayed to see what had captured his attention. The book on how to read Tarot cards was prominently displayed, and I knew I hadn't put it there. Who would have done that? I flashed to that single mocking brow, raised so perfectly and knew. Damn, Quinn. Time for damage control.

"Do you believe you can read the future or is it an act?" Jason asked, flipping through the pages.

I sighed. "I think for most readers it's an act. They learn to watch people, ask questions, and then answer the questions vaguely or use the client's own desires to predict happiness. There's no harm in it. Everyone walks away happy in the end."

"But what about you, KC? Is that how you do it? *Do you tell fortunes at the Honey House?*" Jason asked. His eyes were full of disappointment.

Suddenly fed up, I said, "Look, Jason, I don't owe you any explanations. It's not like we're in a long-term relationship and I've been lying to you. We're just getting to know each other. Before I took over the Honey House, I was a psychic for a cruise line, providing entertainment through fortune telling. Sometimes I had a little luck and could *"see"* something about the client that was different from the regular reading." I made little air quotes to emphasize my point. "If I saw something, I shared it with them. That's all. It was entertainment."

"And is it all entertainment?" he asked softly. "Will you read for me, KC?"

I shrugged. I could see that tonight was going to hell in a hand basket. Journalist Jason was on the scene. My "maybe" place had turned into a big fat "not-tonight-and-probably-not-ever-in-this-lifetime" place.

"Give me your hand, and I'll try." I held my hands out expectantly, and he placed a hand in mine. Instantly there was a flare, and I knew I *would* be able to read him. Closing my eyes, I pulled my hands back slightly from his and let the heat rise. I don't know how else to describe it. I held my hands, palm facing palm, about three inches apart, and Jason's hand hovered between mine. Images and impressions flashed in my mind. "You have one brother, and someone else. Maybe a half sister? I can't see your mom, but your dad is still important to you." I concentrated a bit more, there wasn't much there, almost as though after asking me to read, he'd changed his mind now and was hiding from me.

"This newspaper job is important to you. The article that you're writing about the sweat lodges is an audition, of sorts. That's why you want it to be so much more, why you're digging."

I quit talking and worked at not reaching out, but rather letting any other impressions flow over me. Suddenly, the images came, a fast-forward slide show. I had a quick image of Jason holding a newspaper, with his article and byline above the fold: Juniper Springs Hoax. Another image appeared of Jason under the bright moonlight, standing alone on the giant boulders that edged the eastern boundary of the Honey House property. A blur of motion as something hit him and took him down. Jason on the ground, his body broken, blood everywhere. Then nothing, just a great blackness. *Aw, shit. I hate when I see bad things.*

The connection between us went cold and dark. The red-hot connection was doused so abruptly that my hands actually felt icy, and I rubbed them against my legs to warm them.

Jason laughed, a little self-conscious sound before dropping his hand to his side. "So," he said. "I guess I got my answer." He wore an expression I'd not seen from him yet. Was that bitterness twisting his handsome face?

My stomach hurt and my head pounded with sudden tension. What was it that I'd seen? What was that blackness? What had attacked him? All of my other visions had been fairly straightforward when they'd come. This one had started that way and then went downhill fast.

"What answer do you think you got, Jason?" I asked quietly.

"That it's complete bullshit. Just like every other story I've looked into around here, it's all bullshit. Every bit of information you told me is publicly available. You just find out who your mark is, gather as much information as possible, and then feed it back in a spooky setting."

I was starting to get pissed. Mostly because he was partially right. That *was* how fortune-telling scams were run. I just happened not to be pulling one.

"Jason, I didn't research you ahead of time and that stuff about your family and job just came to me. I told you it doesn't work every time. Just with some people. And it wasn't all I saw," I added reluctantly.

He held up his hand in a stop gesture. "Don't say any more, KC. I really don't want to hear it. Next thing you're going to tell me is I'm going to meet a dangerous stranger or take a voyage. Just stop. I don't think I'm the right man for you. I don't have the stomach for lies."

Stung, my eyes blazed with tears. "I think it's best for you to go now."

"Yeah," he said. "I've got a story to write."

Chapter Four

It had been several days since Gabrielle's dinner party, and I was no closer to answers about why I was here. My mornings all started the same way. I made coffee, brought out the breakfast trays, and sat staring into my mug, waiting for the caffeine buzz to hit. Quinn would arrive a few minutes later, throw the paper on *his* table, pour a cup of coffee, and sit for an uninterrupted hour of reading, sipping, and eating.

This morning there was an edge to Quinn.

"Miss Carmichael," he said on his way to the coffee.

"Sheriff," I replied. We'd never given up our formal titles for each other. I think we both thought the distance was as comfortable as we would ever be with each other. Gabrielle said it was sexy as hell. *Whatever.*

I was just contemplating sneaking off for another hour of sleep when the front section of the Sunday paper landed unceremoniously on my table. I jumped and my coffee sloshed, splashing the front page.

"What the hell? Watch what you're doing," I practically snarled. Mornings were not my best time to be social.

"Read it," he said.

I opened my mouth to protest, took one look at Quinn's unyielding face, and knew he wouldn't relent until I looked at whatever it was he wanted me to see.

It was Jason's article. *Wow!* He'd made the front page, above the fold, and had a byline. *Good for him.* Even if it was a slow news day, this was a big break. Then the headline penetrated my morning brain. HAVEN for HOAXES—

I flipped the paper and saw a small photograph of the *Welcome to Juniper Springs* sign and a picture of the sweat lodge. Showcasing the two images together seemed a bit harsh.

I started reading, expecting the article to be a rehash of the Ted Sparks scandal, and in some ways, it was. Jason began with a brief history of Ted and his *Mecca for the Chosen Ones* retreat.

The article explained that Native Americans had used sweat lodges in ancient and sacred rituals meant only for them. Sparks had bastardized the process by building his own version of a sweat lodge, using concrete blocks and heavy canvass. He charged his followers between five and ten thousand dollars a person to crowd into the 400-square foot structure, where his flunkies would stoke the fire while Ted chanted self-actualization nonsense. Two hours later the faithful would emerge, spiritually and financially cleansed. Last summer, four people died and twenty more were hospitalized from severe heat stroke. Sparks was in prison awaiting trial.

The article was well written, infusing the right amount of facts and personal accounts by the victims to draw the reader in. I thought Jason had done a bang up job, until I got to the conclusion:

Ted Sparks was not the only business in town to profit from the exploitation of others. A recent spate of reported paranormal activity has brought throngs of tourists to the small community of Juniper Springs. Business is thriving for those operating ghost sighting tours of cemeteries and burial grounds. People wait weeks and pay thousands of dollars for a "Vortex infusion," a type of blood exchange with an allegedly supernatural being.

Even the local bed and breakfast seems to be in on the act. The prognosticating proprietor is an ex-convict and a member of a family long associated with perpetrating fraud on unsuspecting victims for profit. Her close ties to

the local sheriff may prevent anyone from examining her activities too closely, but there is speculation she will soon be operating a fortune-telling scheme from her hostelry.

Over the next six weeks I will bring you stories of some of these businesses and expose how the operators use the increasing interest in paranormal activities to trick otherwise sensible people into parting with their hard earned cash.

Next week: A look at "The Way They Were," a hunting lodge that purports to take guests on a photo safari of actual werewolves.

Slumping against the back of the chair, I stared numbly at the paper for a long time after I finished reading. I don't know how Jason had found out about my juvenile record, but to call me an ex-con in the press was harsh. The only person whose fortune I'd read was his, and Lord knows I did not have a relationship with the local sheriff.

"Seems your boyfriend likes to kiss and tell, Miss Carmichael. Where is Jason this morning? In town and back in your bed?" Quinn's voice vibrated with anger.

"He's not my boyfriend. We had one date at the dinner party, and I haven't seen or heard from him since. No thanks to you."

Quinn blinked. Whatever he was expecting, it hadn't been that.

"What exactly do I have to do with whether your boyfriend wants to see you?"

"You know what you did. Going into my apartment and putting the book on fortune telling on the coffee table? Once he saw that, he was no longer interested in me."

"I have no idea what you're talking about. Other than the night I showed you around the building, I've never been in your apartment. You need to find a way to control your boyfriend. I don't care if he reports on the sweat lodges, but you keep him away from any reporting about wereanimals of any kind."

I stared at Quinn, momentarily speechless. Through a jaw so tightly tensed it might shatter at any moment, I ground out, "He is not my boyfriend. I do not have any contact with him, and I wouldn't control him, even if I could." I took a deep calming breath. "Why would you care if Jason writes about werewolves? No one can seriously believe they exist. People who pay to see something like that know it's as fake as a haunted house at Halloween. They're paying to be entertained. No one is that gullible.

"What in the hell are you so upset over, anyway, Sheriff? It's me he's trashed. He told the world I have a record, about my family. I don't do fortune telling, and I don't con people. It's just a bed and breakfast, and I didn't do anything to get caught up in any of this."

I threw the paper down on the table and went to refill my coffee. When I turned around, Quinn was gone.

The phone rang, and my voice was sharp when I answered.

"Hey, beautiful, don't kill the messenger." Gregory's voice was warm and full of laughter. I think Gregory's voice would be warm and full of laughter if he told you your house was on fire. He was just one of those people who saw life through the funny pages.

"Hey, Gregory. Sorry I snapped. What's up?"

"Well, I'm guessing from the sound of your voice that you already saw your boyfriend's article?" There was a distinct edge to his smart-assed comment. *Huh.* Maybe not so sunny after all?

"Yes, the sheriff was kind enough to throw it in my face this morning. And Jason isn't my boyfriend."

"Did you fuck him? Cause he sure fucked you!"

"Gregory!" I could hear Owen's outraged voice echoing mine in the background.

"Sorry, KC. It's just that—" He broke off, and I heard him breathing. It sounded as though he'd just finished running. Okay, definitely not the funny papers today. This was all very un-Gregory-like behavior.

There was a long pause, but by the time he responded, his momentary show of temper seemed to be easing back. "I'm sorry, KC. I started this badly, I'm not angry with you. Owen and I would really appreciate it if you could talk to Jason. See if you can convince him to stick with the sweat lodges and palmistry. Hell, we'll even throw in a couple of really good frauds we know about that are closer to Sedona. People will eat it up. You know they love to hear about the rich and lazy getting swindled. Just keep him out of Juniper Springs."

I was silent for a few moments, wondering what I was missing. So I asked, "What am I missing, Gregory? He didn't mention G&O at all. What would organic grocers have to worry about?"

"Aww, KC, don't be daft. We just don't want the press all over here, digging around, that's all. Talk to him, okay, hun?"

"No," I said. "Jason isn't my boyfriend, he never was. He obviously holds no special place for me, since he alluded to my less than illustrious past. Personally, he could get hit by a truck tomorrow, and I wouldn't care. You want to talk to him? Be my guest. You might have to line up behind the sheriff, though. He was pretty pissed himself this morning."

"Mmmmm," Gregory made yummy sounds, the good humor back in his voice. Had to give the man credit—at least when he had hissy fits they seemed to be short-lived. "I'd love to line up behind Quinn. All that tall, tan, and handsome. I don't think I'm exactly his type. Okay, love, can't blame a man for trying. Are we still on for our run tomorrow morning?"

"Sure. I hate it," I laughed, "but I'll be ready."

We hung up on a good note, but the phone rang almost immediately. In fact, the phone continued to ring virtually non-stop for the rest of the morning. It seemed that the owner of just about every business in town expected me to be able to stop Jason's articles. Eventually, I took the phone off the hook, turned off my cell phone, and tried to yoga my way into a peaceful afternoon.

It wasn't until the front door opened that I realized just how impossible that was going to be.

A woman entered and stood looking around, practically quivering with excitement. She was shorter than my five feet five inches, and outweighed me by at least sixty pounds. With her tight, red perm, she looked like a sixty-year old Little Orphan Annie on steroids. Her arms and neck were covered with necklaces and bracelets of silver, leather, turquoise, and beads. Even with all of that to look at, it was still the neon yellow caftan that overwhelmed the visual senses.

"Hello! Is this the only bed and breakfast in Juniper Springs?" she trilled.

"Yes," I said. I had a sinking feeling that I knew where this was going.

"Lovely. May I have a room, please?"

Mentally rolling my eyes, I wanted to tell her no. I knew she was here because of the article. She was looking for a genuine paranormal experience and she would be expecting to meet the fortuneteller. Maybe I could tell her we were booked. Gabrielle was off until tomorrow, she'd never know.

As soon as the thought entered my mind, I felt the shift in the atmosphere of the house. The air settled around me just as it had the first time I entered the Honey House and a small shiver ran up my spine. I remembered Gabrielle's words: no one comes into the House for a room who isn't supposed to be here. With a long-suffering sigh, I led the way to a vacant room.

As the day progressed, at least a dozen other people stopped by to look at Honey House, take pictures and walk around the grounds. None of them asked for rooms, but the House seemed pleased by the attention. Doors I'd previously closed mysteriously opened so the tourists could get a peek inside. The fountain in the courtyard began to flow, and everything sparkled. There was a definite sense of well-being hovering in the air. *Weird.*

On the ship, I'd spent late afternoons and evenings giving readings for the fun-loving passengers. Some were serious, some were light-hearted, and none was physically taxing. I would dance and make the tourists happy with harmless flirtations. Sometimes it was a little more than flirting, but not too often. I kept in shape by running and taking a mixed martial arts class.

Tonight, I would be lucky to drag myself to the bed upstairs. Who knew that giving tours, posing for pictures, and dodging requests for psychic readings could be so exhausting?

I went to check the front door, to make sure it was locked for the night. Just as I reached out, the door swung open and there was Jason.

"May I come in?" he asked tentatively.

"Are you here for a room?" *Please say no, please say no, please say no.*

"Yes," he answered softly. He wouldn't meet my eyes.

Another important life lesson: never be afraid to meet your enemy's eyes. Otherwise, you'll never see what's coming.

I invited him inside and shut the door. Without any hesitation, I drove my fist into his stomach. He hunched over, trying to draw a breath and I grabbed his shoulders, forcing him to double over and drove his face into my knee.

Jason moaned in a ball on the floor. Sucking on a scraped knuckle—damn belt buckle—I gathered the sheets and towels for his room and stacked them on the floor near his head, along with a room key. Then I went to bed and slept like a baby.

****

The early morning run wasn't going exactly as planned. "For Christ's sake, move over, Gregory," I said as I shoved him off the path. Gregory wasn't laughing now. He was bent over, hands propped on his knees, throat working. He was making a horrible gagging sound. If anything was going to make me puke, it would be listening to those wet heaves, not the bloody body blocking the path.

I called for the sheriff and an ambulance before I knew whether the body was alive. I would be too bloody to hold the phone once I moved in close enough to check for a pulse. There was no level of first aid that would make a difference, even *if* whoever was underneath all that blood was still alive. The best I could do was offer comfort.

I answered the dispatcher's questions then handed the phone to a very green looking Gregory. "Stay on the line, Gregory, but step over there. Don't watch if you're going to get sick. I'll tell you if I can feel a pulse and you can tell the dispatcher."

I carefully stepped onto the driest spot possible and reached past the collar to lay my fingers against the cool flesh. There was a thready beat against my fingers and I relayed the information. Then I tried to see if any wounds were bleeding copiously and needed pressure to stop the flow. It looked as though most of the blood was pooled on the ground already.

Through it all I murmured reassurances. "It's okay, you're going to be all right. What's your name, hon? You're going to be all right."

I was pretty sure the body was a man. He was curled on his side in a fetal position, knees tucked tight against his stomach. The jeans and windbreaker were coated with blood and the red sandy dirt of the trail. The hair was matted, and caked in that Sedona red earth. The face was torn open, cut from the mandible to the left temple, and showed bone. If he survived, he would have one hell of a story to tell. The skin where I laid my fingers against his neck was cold, and I knew shock was as deadly as anything else he faced right now. I draped my jacket lightly over his shoulders and waited for the ambulance.

****

"Tell me once more how you found the victim, Miss Carmichael? Why did you vary your usual route this morning?" I sighed. Once again, Quinn took up entirely too much space. I looked at the couch cushions and he was only taking one-third of the couch. I was curled up on my cushion at the opposite end and there was still one full cushion between us. So why did it feel as though he was looming over me?

"I already answered that, Sheriff. Twice. We were running. It's only the third time that Gregory and I have run together. We don't have a usual route. I don't know why we ran up the back path, we just did. Now, unless you have new questions for me, I have things to do around here."

Quinn stared at me a long time. Cop eyes. I hated cop eyes. "Why didn't you tell me Jason was back in town?" he asked.

I blinked, momentarily nonplussed by the sudden shift in the conversation. Heat crawled up my neck at the memory of what I'd done last night. *Shit.* I used to give much better blank face than that. Oh well, it couldn't be helped now.

"I didn't tell you, Sheriff, because it's none of your business," I said coolly. I made to move and Quinn was suddenly there, practically on top of me. He grabbed my wrist in a painfully tight grip.

"Not yet, Miss Carmichael. Tell me about Jason Brill."

I stared at his hand until he finally dropped my wrist, but one look at his face told me he was not going to drop the question.

"Jason showed up last night, just before the door locked. He asked for a room. I gave him a key. End of story." I clipped the words. I so did not want to go there with Quinn.

"Did you fuck him?"

"What? No!"

"What time did he arrive?"

The questions were coming fast now. I was familiar with the technique. The sheriff would pose rapid-fire questions and buried somewhere in the midst was the real question he wanted answered. He hoped to catch me off-guard and it had almost worked. I deliberately slowed the pace, pausing before answering, as though it required great effort of thought.

"Nine," I said.

His phone rang and he answered, "Quinn." After listening a few minutes he ended the call with a promising, "I'll be right there."

"Last chance, Miss Carmichael. Is there anything else you want to tell me about Mr. Brill?"

"No. I don't know why you'd think Jason and I are any of your business, anyway," I responded. Then I gave myself a mental kick for giving the cop the opening he was looking for. He surprised me. He didn't jump at it, just looked at me, his big honey-colored eyes filled with some emotion I didn't understand.

Quinn reached a hand, and I let him pull me to my feet. I schooled my face against any sign of discomfort as he ran his thumb over the slightly swollen and abraded knuckles of my right hand. "You'll have to tell me who you hit when I return," he said softly.

I think it was the tone. It was the first time today he'd spoken to me as though I was a person and not an ex-con. My eyes filled unexpectedly with tears, and I turned away, pulling my hand from his. Staring blindly out the window, I felt Quinn as he stepped close to me. His body threw off heat, a pulsing energy, as though he were a sun and I was forced into his orbit. I wanted to step away, but couldn't. I was glad he was behind me; I didn't want to see the look on his face.

"Jason Brill died a few minutes ago. He was too badly injured. The doctors couldn't do anything. I'm sorry," he added softly.

My knees buckled. Quinn caught me and carried me to the couch. That bloody thing had been Jason? I hadn't even recognized him. I'd let him die alone.

I asked, as if needing to hear the words, to watch his face, "That was *Jason*? Dear God, what happened? It looked as though he'd been eaten."

My mind flashed to the image I'd had of him when I'd performed the reading. Jason flying through the air. That awful blackness. Had I somehow foreseen this? Could I have prevented this if I'd told him what I'd seen?

Quinn looked at me, his face solemn. "It was Jason. I need to go. Will you be all right alone, or should I send Gabrielle in?"

"I'm all right. I just need some time."

He nodded, passed a surprisingly gentle hand across my forehead, smoothing my hair away from my face, then left.

Chapter Five

The woman wore a neon green caftan today and had decorated herself in coral and silver jewelry. The contrast was startling between the two, and she brought to mind a giant parrot. *Scary.* She hovered as I busied myself around the great room, and it wasn't long before she made her intentions clear.

"I've been waiting until the hubbub died down to speak with you, dear," she chirped in my direction. "I wonder if I might have a reading today?"

"Listen, Mrs. Kensington, this just isn't a good day for me. Besides, I don't do readings anymore."

"Oh, but darling, you must. We have so much to talk about," she said.

Why is it people don't want to take no for an answer? They think they can just rephrase the question and despite any of your misgivings, you'll suddenly say, "Sure, I'd love to." Well, I wouldn't love to. I'd let Jason talk me into it and I'd seen something. Something remarkably similar to the reality of his bloodied and beaten body. I never wanted to *"see"* anything again. I needed to be polite; after all, she was a guest of the Honey House. On the other hand, no means no. She needed to accept that I wasn't going to do a psychic reading for her.

"I'm really sorry you're disappointed, Mrs. Kensington, but I won't read for you or anybody. Would you like me to ask Gabrielle if she knows of any good psychics in the area?"

"Oh, child. You really don't understand. Please, let's find some privacy. I have a great deal to tell you."

"About what?" I was being less than polite, but I didn't want to be tied up in a conversation about palmistry all afternoon. I needed time to sort through my thoughts about Jason. Plus, I knew Quinn would eventually return to ask more questions than he'd asked this morning.

Up until now, I'd taken Mrs. Kensington as a piece of tourist fluff, a woman completely absorbed by her own interests. Now, I was forced to reevaluate my initial impressions. Somehow, she'd pulled energy like a cloak around her. Her shoulders lowered and chin rose, so that she looked positively regal. She looked at me a long minute and it made me feel young, caught in the act even though I'd done nothing wrong. I was uncomfortably reminded that the House wouldn't have let her stay if it hadn't wanted her here.

"We really must talk. Joanne was a friend of mine. There are things you need to know. Please, can we go somewhere private?"

Surprising myself with the offer, I said, "Let's go into the library."

The library was a wonder. Located in the exact opposite corner of the House from my apartment, it caught the afternoon sunlight. Joanne's books covered two walls, floor to ceiling. I loved to read, and I'd intended to spend a great deal of time in here when I first saw the room. So far, the details of running a bed and breakfast had consumed me. Looking around, I was reminded of the attraction.

"Please, have a seat," the woman said, as if this was her place, not mine. She indicated two low-slung leather and wood chairs that faced catty-corner in front of the large window that held a spectacular view of one of the more famous red-rock formations. The kind you usually only saw on post cards.

I sat and waited for her to begin. She had certainly aroused my curiosity.

"Have you found Joanne's Book of Shadows?" she asked without preamble.

"Book of Shadows?" I repeated.

"Yes," she nodded. "It's a book used by the Wiccan and witches to record their work and research. Joanne's contained a list of her herbs and their uses, the moon cycles, our Sabbats and holidays, and even her spells. I take it you haven't found it?"

"Joanne was a witch?" I asked. Without waiting for an answer, I pressed on. "Mrs. Kensington—"

"Please, call me Amelia," she interrupted.

"All right. Amelia. Why are you here?" I asked, cutting to the chase.

"The question, child, is why are *you* here? You're a very unusual young woman, KC," Amelia said.

I waited. She sighed. I waited some more.

"Either you are remarkably uncurious or you have iron control over your nerves. I wonder. You know, I never thought you'd come. When Joanne returned from the cruise, she told me all about you. She was quite impressed with your innate power, although she reiterated you were barely aware of it yourself. I didn't believe that could possibly be true, but I see now that she was right.

"I was surprised when Joanne told me the House had selected you. An untrained power unleashed in the House, let loose in this part of the world is a frightening thought for an old woman. Joanne would know, though. Honestly, I expected you would ignore the request when Malcolm came to get you from the ship. I certainly never imagined you would move in that very day and not return to your old life. Why is that? What made you so willing to give everything up to come here? Do you feel compelled, child?"

Did I feel compelled? I suppose in a way I did. This was a life that was far different from any I had known. This was a life with "normal" written all over it. I had a home, a job, and I was even starting to make friends.

"I don't know if I can explain it well, Amelia," I said, wondering why I was explaining at all. "I've lived mostly as a nomad, with no real roots, no real connection to anything. I came with lawyer-boy, er, Malcolm on a lark. I figured Joanne was trying to lure me here to be her pet faux fortuneteller, to help drum up more business for her bed and breakfast. I never imagined for a minute that she was really dead. When I got here, something about the place got to me. I still didn't believe, but I saw Joanne's, uhm, ghost?" My voice rose as if in question.

I was really squirming now. When I had arrived, nothing could have persuaded me to share this experience, but I suppose Amelia hit the nail on the head. I did feel compelled. Compelled to share with her, compelled to stay. I took a deep breath and continued.

"I saw Joanne's ghost, except I still wondered how she was pulling it off, what the scam was. I had no reason to go back to the ship; I had plenty of savings to last a while and a place to stay, so I thought, why not stay and see what happens next?

"Somehow, I just keep getting sucked deeper. I still don't really believe I own the House. Partly because I've never owned anything and partly because it seems wrong to think of this place as capable of being owned. It's fascinating. People just show up, we don't advertise, they're just suddenly here. I don't know what I'm trying to say," I added, and I could hear the frustration in my own voice.

Amelia smiled then, a smile full of knowledge and almost pride. It was as though I had mastered some particularly difficult skill, and Amelia was proud of me. I hated secrets. Her smile made me feel left out of whatever knowledge she had that I lacked. She wanted me to ask, to seek her superior knowledge. I wouldn't. She wouldn't be able to keep her secret, people seldom could.

"The House did pick you. It picks all of us, but has very few other real powers. The real power, my dear, is within you. Most of us that the House picks are aware of the power within, but we need training and a safe harbor. You truly seem unaware of that which roils beneath your surface. I imagine the House is energized by you."

"What are you saying, Amelia? Are you telling me you think the House is yours, too?" I asked edgily. Was she trying to move in here permanently?

"Oh, dear child, put your back down. I explain myself poorly. I was the owner before Joanne. I have no need of the House now. No, the House has chosen you, and now it's up to you to discover the power that makes you special. I am a witch. Oh, there. Now I've shocked you."

"No, I'm all right," I said. "Please, tell me more. How did you come to own the House? And you're not dead, so how did Joanne get it?"

"Well, it has been a long time since I owned it. The owner before me was named Syvia. She found me one day as I was passing through Sedona on my way to Flagstaff to the teacher's college there. There weren't as many jobs available to independent young women back then as there are today. Regardless, I stayed at the House for one night. The House took a shine to me, and before I knew it, Syvia offered me a job running the place and she left for what she told me was a safari. I never did find out where she really went. Two days after she was gone, an attorney presented me with the deed and the place was suddenly mine."

I gasped. That was very similar to my own experience and said so.

"Yes, it's the way of the House. I knew it was time for me to go when Joanne and I quite literally ran into each other. I had gone to Phoenix on an errand and we bumped into each other passing through the door to an herbalist's shop. She was interested in witchcraft and was just starting her Book of Shadows. She'd gone to the herbalist to learn about alchemy. I invited her to the House and when it was time, I transferred it to her."

"So the House just decides when it's time for the owner to move on? Then what happened to Joanne? Is she really dead? Because I saw her ghost. Didn't I?"

"Oh, yes. She's quite dead. But that had nothing to do with the House, dear. Just because Joanne has passed to the other side doesn't mean she can't still visit from time-to-time. I'm sure she was just helping the House, doing a little playacting to give you a push in the right direction."

She paused to let me absorb all that she'd told me so far. I wasn't sure what to ask next. Was I supposed to be a witch? Is that what she was trying to tell me? I wanted to know, so I asked her.

Amelia smiled and leaned forward to pat my hand. "Oh, it is far from me to predict where your talents will emerge." With a final squeeze, she leaned back before continuing. "Joanne wanted to be a witch, and so she was. I had ideas to be a teacher. Once I moved here, I kept meeting powerful witches, and each of them saw something in me and taught me. Syvia was a powerful psychic. Each of us has a special talent. Be patient, dear.

Yours will emerge. You already demonstrate some awareness of the other dimension and psychic abilities. Keep yourself open to possibilities beyond what you know now. Turn no one away from the House.

Brushing her hands over her lap, Amelia looked toward the window for a moment. KC had the absurd notion the woman was listening to something only she could hear. Turning back, she smiled again, but it looked a little forced. "That's all for now, dear. I'm tired. I have two things for you before I leave. First, find Joanne's Book of Shadows. I don't know where she kept it, but it's critical we not let it leave the House. It could be dangerous in the wrong hands."

I knew she wanted to go, but I still had questions. I sat up a little straighter...not exactly easy in the low-slung chair. "Can you explain more about the Book of Shadows?" I asked.

"It's the collection of all of Joanne's work. It's where she stored all the information about her magickal traditions; it's an item of power. She should also have her Grimoire, her spell book, stored nearby. Combined, the two books contain a tremendous amount of information and should not be seen by anyone other than you."

I think I must have blinked funny, because she laughed a little. "KC, you should keep your own Book of Shadows, while you're still learning about your powers. Even if you don't become a witch, it's an excellent idea for you to develop your own traditions and rituals."

Pushing up from the chair, I crossed the room and looked back at Amelia. "You said two things. What's the other thing I need to know? Or is it the other thing I need to do?" I asked.

"Very astute. You need to become closer to the House. Ask it why you are here; test what I have told you so far. You will sense I am telling you the truth. The House will not hurt you. It is here to bring a great power to the Earth, and that power lies within you. Go ahead," she said. "Try it now, reach out. Think about the House and yourself. See if you can sense that I'm telling you the truth."

Turning away from her, I looked out the window, at the shadows stretching across the yard. I wasn't sure I wanted to know if this was the truth. It seemed more palatable when I thought this was an elaborate scam by Joanne. Now Amelia was telling me this was all part of some cosmic plot to bring me here so I could learn of some yet to be defined power within me. Was this way too woowoo, even for me?

Tentatively, I stretched out my senses to see if I could tell anything about the House. I was prepared to be freaked out, to demand my freedom and run screaming from the House. I wasn't prepared for the feelings that washed through me. Calm and light, and sense of destiny. *I was home.*

When I turned to tell Amelia, she was gone and Quinn stood in her place.

"Miss Carmichael," he said. "I need to see Jason's room."

Abruptly drawn back into the reality of the day, I nodded. I led Quinn next door to Jason's suite, and used the master key from my ring to unlock the door. Quinn placed his hand on my arm, stilling the movement. He took over and unlatched the door himself. I noticed he had his right hand on the butt of his gun, the strap unsnapped.

When he drew his gun, I reversed direction until my back hit the cool plaster of the hallway wall. It hadn't occurred to me that someone might be waiting inside. I was really slow on the uptake on this one.

Quinn made a gesture with his hand that I took to mean, "Wait here," and stepped to the doorway. He sighted his gun around the room, then entered cautiously, leaving the door partially opened behind him. He verified the closet, bathroom, and under the bed were all free from intruders, then invited me inside. The room was blank, no imprint of Jason had been made upon the space.

****

KC,

When I started investigating this article, I was convinced everything was a hoax. Not anymore. Some of it is, but not all. I'm about to change the world here, and it scares the shit out of me.

I'll be leaving sometime tomorrow, but first, as the saying goes, I have to see a man about a dog. I'm more sorry than I can possibly say for the things in the article about you and your family. I think I can fix the damage to you, if you'll let me, but we need to talk. I know I don't deserve it, but please give me a second chance. I'll share what I've learned. I expected to have more control over things. Now I just don't know.

JB

I fingered the paper, tracing the cramped cursive, imagining Jason hurriedly scratching the note and leaving it in my room. It had been propped on the mantle with my initials scrawled on the front, waiting for me to take notice. Jason must have come in while I was putting out the coffee or after I left to run with Gregory this morning. That meant it was one of the last things he'd done before he was killed. Before he was murdered, I corrected. Quinn had been very clear on that point, that someone had murdered Jason. From the way he was asking questions, it seemed he thought I was a likely candidate.

It would certainly be a popular solution if Quinn could tie me to the murder. Stranger with a criminal record comes to town; intrepid reporter who outs said criminal is murdered. A very neat formula, if you ask me. Of course, I *knew* I hadn't killed Jason, which meant there was a murderer running around Juniper Springs. I would need to find the real murderer before Quinn put me in the starring role.

Chapter Six

"Going to see a man about a dog. What the hell could that mean?" I asked for the third time. Owen just looked at me, his soft gray eyes amused.

"What?" I asked, frustration coloring my voice.

"KC, I told you already. It's just a saying meaning you need to talk with someone. I'm sure Jason didn't mean he literally needed to talk about a dog. He might not have even meant he was going to talk to a man. It's just a saying," he repeated.

Gregory pushed open the French doors with his hip and stepped outside carrying an enormous platter of appetizers to the low-slung patio table. It was my first time at their home and just being here made me feel good. It suited them perfectly. The house was actually a private extension of their store, with the kitchen, dining, and living rooms downstairs, and two bedrooms and an office, plus a lot of storage upstairs. The backyard was an abundance of flowers and herbs, and we sat on the patio watching the sun turn a fiery red, as though angry at being forced to move along and cede its glory to the night.

Snatching a crab stuffed mushroom from the tray, I forced my eyes not to roll back in their sockets from sheer joy at the treat. *Yum.* "Oh God, Gregory, these are delicious. Do you use that oven-thingy to make them?" I asked, only half joking. Cooking was one of many normal skills my foster parents hadn't bothered with teaching me.

Laughing, Gregory said, "Yes, I used an *oven-thingy.* So can you. All you have to do is heat and serve."

"Gregory makes them himself and we sell a big batch of them each week. One batch only, so if you want some, you'd better place an order. Gregory makes several of our specialty items. We don't advertise them, but you can get a list. It's beyond a doubt the best food in the valley. Several of the local restaurants have tried to lure him away, but he likes the freedom of deciding what to make and when," Owen said.

"Well, look at you all puffed up and proud," I said to Owen, but he only had eyes for Gregory. The men exchanged tender smiles, before turning back to me.

"What do you eat, KC? I mean other than the breakfast stuff from here. Do you cook?" Gregory asked.

"I cook, sometimes," I said, sounding defensive, even to myself.

"What's the last thing you cooked?" Gregory challenged.

"Uhm...ramen?" I offered.

"Seriously, KC," Gregory gave a derisive snort, "I don't think I've seen you in the store, lately. What did you have for dinner last night?"

"Leftovers," I said brightly, pleased to have an answer that would let me slip out of this embarrassing conversation.

Gregory narrowed his eyes. "Leftover what?"

Shit. With I sigh, I admitted, "A yogurt and bagel left over from breakfast."

Once Gregory stopped laughing, he retrieved an order form from the kitchen. "This is what I'm making next week. Appetizers, chicken, and wild rice soup, and I think for you I'll add a big field greens salad. I cook on Mondays, so the food will be with your Tuesday morning delivery. I'll send some real leftovers from dinner tonight over in the morning, so you don't starve between now and Tuesday. Owen, honey, will you make sure that gets put into KC's order in the morning?"

Owen's eyes sparkled at his lover's mothering. "Congratulations, KC, on becoming Gregory's latest stray. I'm afraid there's no peace for you, now. Before you know it, he'll know everything there is to know about Katherine Carmichael. Hell, he's gonna want to approve your dates from now on."

It was my turn to snort. "Even if I was interested in dating, the prospects are pretty slim pickings. The only ones that have shown any interest in me are you two…and well, you're both already taken." I smiled, and then quickly changed the subject.

"So what do you think Jason meant?" I asked, worrying at the question once more.

"What did Quinn say?" Owen asked.

I said nothing, but Gregory gasped. "You bad thing! You didn't tell the big, old sheriff, did you? He is one seriously fine piece of man. Too bad Quinn doesn't swing this way. He would certainly warm up a cold winter night. Do you think he's as big as that faded patch on his jeans makes him out to be?"

"What patch?" I asked innocently. Of course, I knew exactly what faded patch he was talking about. Quinn hung seriously left. "The sheriff and I have a mutual understanding. He doesn't like me and I don't like him. Besides, I think Susan might object."

Gregory and Owen both laughed good-naturedly.

"There's no love lost between the two of them. Susan has been trying to get her hands on him ever since he arrived. He's the original artful dodger," Gregory said. "In fact, I don't actually know where he gets his itch scratched. He plays up to Susan when there's a social need, but really, he treats all the women with the same aloofness. But he doesn't set off my gaydar either. He's certainly not asexual. No, it's definitely women, and personally I think the little bristle thing between the two of you is just stoking the fire. Eventually, the two of you will ignite."

"Not going to happen, Romeo," I said to Gregory. "He's not my type."

"What type is that?" Owen asked.

"Not a cop." When the laughter settled I went right back to where my thoughts had been all day. "Okay, you two, truth between us. Did Jason come to visit you for his article series?"

With a sigh, Owen said, "You aren't going to let this go, are you?"

"Nope. And no prevaricating. Did Jason interview you or try to interview you?"

They exchanged a long look before Gregory finally answered. "Yes. He interviewed Owen the first visit. Since we don't do anything with the paranormal trade, neither of us was particularly worried about what he might ask. He asked some background questions, trying to get some local color. It wasn't any big deal."

There was just a flicker of his eyes. Down and to the right, just for an instant before returning unflinching to meet my gaze. It was a tell. I'd play poker with Gregory any day of the week. He was lying.

"Was that the only time you spoke with him?"

"Yes, it was the only time he was here." Again, Gregory answered for the both of them.

"Did he ever call either of you?"

Owen sighed, and I knew he'd just decided to tell me something he hadn't wanted to.

"He called, KC. He called a couple of times. He wanted to know about food deliveries to the Were Ranch."

"The Way They Were?" I confirmed. When they both nodded, I sat back and nibbled on another mushroom, and looked at them expectantly.

"Look, KC. All he wanted to know was how much food they ordered and how it got to the ranch. It's a weekly order; they pick it up. No big deal. Now, let's go eat dinner." Gregory led the way inside.

As we sat down to a scrumptious meal of grilled salmon and artichokes, my one-track mind hit overdrive. "Who else did Jason interview?"

"Your favorite gal-pal, Susan," Gregory answered.

I wrinkled my nose. I wouldn't look forward to talking with her. "Anyone else? Did anyone refuse to talk with him?" I asked.

"Well, I don't know if he actually spoke to anyone at the ranch," Owen said slowly. "Just that he wanted to. I think he was going to that new-age palmistry and crystal shop on Main. He said something at the dinner party about Vortex Infusions. And of course, he must have visited the new business by Ted Sparks."

"Wait a minute," I said. "Ted Sparks? The one that was running the sweat lodges? He's in jail, isn't he?"

"Yep," said Gregory. "Awaiting trial, as they say. But, I guess he has to pay for his defense. He's the name behind 'The Rapture.' It's supposed to be a spiritual healing that uses the hidden hot springs. I guess the theory is the same as the sweat lodge. Go squeeze into a hot, over-crowded space and listen to canned messages from the leader. Come out all rosy and inspired to hand even more money over to Sparks and his people.

"Now, if you don't mind, KC, I'd like to talk about something other than scams. So, tell me. How are you loving Juniper Springs? Any desire to go into the big city?"

We spent the rest of the evening drinking a good Pinot Noir, talking about books and movies, and offering our own expert opinions on the personal lives and styles of celebrities. When it was time to go home, I stood, stretched, and declined the offer of a ride. I walked down the path that led through their yard. Looking back at the patio as I closed the gate, I saw that Gregory had moved closer to Owen on the couch, and Owen dropped an arm over the smaller man's shoulders. I envied their closeness. I didn't know what it was like to feel that connection with another. It wasn't sexual. It was comforting, supportive. I sighed and walked home, feeling the kiss of coolness hidden in the breeze.

****

Quinn was waiting when I reached the Honey House. *Swell.* I'd had too much to drink to spar with him. I let a bone-weary sigh carry my thoughts at having him here, before I asked, "What do you want, Sheriff?"

"I have a few more questions, Miss Carmichael. May I come in?"

"Won't it wait until tomorrow? I've had a pleasant evening and I'd like to curl up with a nightcap to relax before I go to bed," I said.

"An excellent suggestion," he said. As he reached around me to grab the door handle the lock snicked open—then Quinn herded me inside. The House and I were going to have to have a talk.

"Actually, I thought I was suggesting we wait until tomorrow."

"And here I thought I would join you for a nightcap." Without waiting for my undoubtedly slack-jawed response, Quinn led the way to my apartment, leaving me to hurry down the hall behind him. It wasn't all bad, since it gave me the opportunity to study 'The Great Behind,' as Gregory liked to call it. It *was* a great ass. But then again, so was the sheriff. A great ass, indeed.

Quinn put his arm out, preventing me from barging into my own apartment. Quietly, he said, "Why don't you let me go through the door first? Just in case." Without waiting for my answer, he went through the doorway, his hand on his weapon.

Shit. Did Quinn think someone was in there? Is that why he was here?

He scanned the downstairs rooms and looked a silent question at me. I nodded my permission for him to check upstairs. I might not like cops, but I wasn't stupid. If Jason's killer was hanging around, I'd let Quinn introduce himself first.

When he'd confirmed that the place was empty of murderers, he walked to the kitchen and unerringly opened the cabinet where I stored the liquor. Of course, it was directly over a small wine rack, so maybe it wasn't that big of a deduction.

"Make yourself at home, Sheriff," I said sarcastically. "How about a drink?"

"Thanks, don't mind if I do." He brought out two glasses, and I heard the bottles shift as he looked over my selection. I was curious to know why he was here and even more curious to see which booze he selected.

He poured us each a generous glass of Macallan, and my estimation of him went up. It was the most expensive bottle in the cabinet. Then he drank his down in a quick gulp and poured another even more generous glass for himself, before he brought my glass to me.

"Care to sit outside, while we talk?" he asked quietly.

His honey-gold eyes were dull with something. Fatigue, maybe? The smart-ass comment died on my tongue. "Sure," I said, and opened the French doors to the deck and led the way. Two steps down, I realized we would be overlooking the path where Jason died. Three steps down I tripped over something that shouldn't have been there.

I looked down and an embarrassingly girly scream ripped from my throat. There was a dead dog stretched out on the third step. A very bloody dead dog.

****

Two hours later, I was huddled on the corner of my couch in front of a fire and sipping another whisky. I'd wrapped a throw around my legs to ward off the chill that had nothing to do with the temperature and everything to do with the day I'd had.

Quinn had been outside ever since we'd found the dog. I knew there were others out there with him, but I hadn't been able to bring myself to go back outside. It was ridiculous to be this upset over a dog. I'd touched the first body I'd found today, and that turned out to be someone I knew. This was some stray or maybe someone's pet, and here I was feeling as if I would cry.

Shit. I brushed at the tear that escaped and closed my eyes to hold back the flood.

I'd learned early enough about being a tough girl, but I felt the self-pity threatening now. After all, not many people are orphaned by the age of three. I wouldn't know the numbers, but I bet even fewer could lay claim to spending two days trapped in a car with their dead family. The site of the accident was discovered because some hikers heard me screaming. I'd learned later that the paramedics had to cut me out of the crumpled steel, still cocooned in my car seat. I didn't actually remember the accident or anything about my birth parents or older brother. Something like that makes a girl tough, right?

After the accident, with no relatives around to claim me, I'd been placed in a group home. I would have stayed there until I was eighteen if the Patterson's hadn't agreed to foster me. So what if my upbringing was unconventional? At least I'd had a home, and by God, I was tough enough to handle this little mess.

As much as I hated to admit it, this situation still had the makings of an elaborate con. Well, except for the dead body. I swiped angrily at the tears and thought about my foster parents. June and Matt Patterson had been running cons for years before they'd brought me into their lives. To their minds, dragging a kid to a scam gave them instant credibility. "Gee, Mrs. Smith, I know we had a meeting set for this morning, but my daughter wasn't feeling too well, so I needed to bring her along. I hope you don't mind." I would flash my deep blue eyes and be polite.

I was taught early never to feel sorry for the mark. It wasn't our fault if a woman was dumb enough to give us her money. And it *was* always a woman. Matt was a fine-looking man who grew more distinguished with age. He always made the pitch and June played the previously satisfied customer who could vouch for his honesty. I played daughter to Matt's heartbroken widower. It was effective as hell.

The last time I'd seen Matt and June was at the Los Angeles County Courthouse nearly ten years ago now. I'd been thirteen and the California Juvenile System became my new family. Six years in lock up at a California Youth Authority farm will either make a girl tough or break her. And damn it all to hell, I was tough, I reminded myself.

Quinn finally came back inside and interrupted my trip down memory lane. I stared into the fire while he poured himself a fresh drink. Neither of us said anything until he joined me on the couch, bringing the bottle with him.

"All right, KC. Everybody's gone, but the photographer will be back in the daylight for another photo. I think we both know this wasn't an accident. Someone is sending a pretty strong message. What is it you're not telling me? Do you know something about Jason's murder? Something else you're holding back?" Quinn asked, his sheriff's mask perfectly in place, his cop eyes blank.

I shook my head. "So these are definitely related?" I asked. Something about that was gnawing at me, but I didn't know what.

"You don't think they are? You can find two bodies in your backyard on the same day and imagine one has nothing to do with the other?"

"I don't know," I answered truthfully.

"Is there someplace I should search besides Jason's room? Did he stay in here with you last night?"

"God, no! After what he wrote about me in the paper?"

"So what? It was all true," Quinn said coldly.

"Just because it's true, doesn't much mean I want others to know. That life is long behind me now."

Quinn smiled a tight smile that didn't change the look in his eyes one iota. "Sounds like a motive for murder. Was it revenge or were there more secrets coming that you don't want known?"

"Fuck off, Sheriff. You don't come into my house, drink my finest whisky, and accuse me of murder." My voice was cold, eyes steady. "You want to charge me? Go ahead. Otherwise, this line of questioning is over."

We stared at each other a long time, but he looked away first. I thought I might have won the skirmish. Then he took my hand and rubbed his thumb gently over the bruised knuckles.

"Will you tell me how this happened?" he asked softly.

I sighed. He was good; I'd give him that. He was playing the bad cop *and* the good cop. I answered him anyway. "I hit Jason. He arrived late and asked for a room. I decked him and dropped the room key by his head. I left him on the floor in the entry. It was the only time I saw him until I found him on the path." I added shakily, "That didn't count because I didn't even recognize him there."

Quinn's eyes sparkled for a minute. "Did you really hit him?" His voice held a hint of something. Laughter? Disbelief?

"Hard enough to knock him out. I'm in pretty good shape, you know," I said. I knew better than to volunteer information to the cops, but I hated it when men assumed any woman was a weak, fragile thing.

Quinn stroked his finger lightly down my arm, tracing a path along the definition of the muscle in my biceps. "I noticed," he said, and something about the smoky richness in his voice made me shiver.

"Do you know whose dog it was?" I blurted, needing a distraction. I'm not sure why it mattered, except I felt vaguely responsible, since it was found on my back porch.

"Not a dog, a coyote," Quinn said. "It wasn't someone's pet, didn't belong to anybody, if that's what you're thinking."

I nodded, not exactly trusting myself to speak. Then the tears started. *Shit.* What was wrong with me?

"Are you all right?" Quinn asked. He slid across the couch and gathered me in his arms, offering temporary comfort where none was expected.

Without thought or reason, I pressed my chest against him and raised my mouth to his.

Chapter Seven

Quinn's lips were a wonder, perfectly shaped, made for kissing, for tasting. I'm not sure which of us was more surprised when my mouth found his, but neither of us turned away. It started as a gentle brush of lips and Quinn stayed very still. Not as though he found it distasteful, more as though he was waiting to see what would happen next. I needed to feel the heat of his tongue, taste his sweetness, hold his breath against mine. He relaxed his mouth against my kiss, and when his lips parted slightly, I pushed inside.

When my tongue found his, Quinn's stillness exploded into a firestorm of desire. He growled at the contact, cupped my face in one large hand while he twisted his fingers roughly into my hair. His desire took control of the kiss and stole my breath. I had a moment to think it was the most extraordinary of kisses before I thought no more. I experienced. I felt. I surrendered.

The dance of our tongues was heated. He plunged into my mouth, sliding against my teeth, my palate, my tongue. I held his tongue with gentle suction, promising acts to come. I followed him back into his own mouth and tasted the whisky, the spice of him, the flavor of us. I wanted more. He pulled his mouth from mine and ran kisses along my jaw line, and then returned to trace my lips, biting gently.

Quinn's tongue followed the line of my collarbone and up the sensitive skin of my neck. He bit down so hard I knew it would leave a mark, but all I could do was arch my neck, make it longer, give him more. His mouth on my neck sent shivers down into the very core of me. I shuddered with anticipation.

I leaned into him at the same time my hands found the buttons on his shirt. I wanted to feel his skin against mine. *Now.*

I unbuttoned his shirt, pulled it from his jeans, and pushed it off his wide shoulders. Quinn leaned forward and wriggled his arms enough to give me room to maneuver. As soon as I bared his chest, I slipped my own shirt over my head and threw it behind me.

His chest was broad, with a patch of dark curls nestled between small coppery nipples. I pulled him back into a kiss with one hand while the other splayed across his chest, nails scraping against the hair. He rubbed his hands against the bare skin of my back, leaving me with the illusion for the briefest of moments that I was driving our pace. Then with a movement so fast that I never saw it coming, he threw me on the couch and stretched out long and hard on top of me.

I felt the grin on my face a second before his mouth claimed mine in another mind-numbing kiss. I liked it a little bit rough, and most men just weren't sure what that meant. I liked my man to be able to stand up to me, to be a little bit dominant in bed. I wanted a man who would seek his pleasure and not be intimidated when I did the same.

Quinn slid his face and hands to my breasts, and I didn't bother to try to disguise the moan he wrenched from me. He disposed of the front closing bra and went straight to work. With a sigh, he pushed my breasts together and ran his tongue along the crease before he began to tease the nipples. Light tongue flicks, a scrape of his teeth, gentle bites on the soft underside. Just as I was sure I couldn't stand anymore teasing, he'd switch to the other breast.

My back arched, impatient, eager for what I knew was coming next. Finally, with another sexy growl, he pulled one nipple into his mouth, while he pinched and rolled the other nipple between his thumb and forefinger. Hard and deep he sucked, and the muscles in my belly and lower clenched tight. A shudder passed through me, a strong precursor of what was to come.

Quinn slid up my body, returning to kiss me with a gentleness he hadn't shown before. His hand caressed my cheek as his mouth pressed against mine. I realized his hair was still bound and I loosened the tie that held it back from his face. Waves of soft golden-brown spilled around us, releasing an earthy scent. I ran my fingers through the silky strands, and he moaned with pleasure against my lips.

"KC…Katherine…Katie." It was as though he was trying my name for the first time and had settled on Katie with a sigh. I'd been Katherine to my parents, and KC in jail. No one had ever called me Katie before. I thought I might like it.

I realized I thought of him as Quinn, but I'd never called him that except for that one bitchy moment in front of Susan. *Quinn.* Short for MacQuinnlan. What was his real first name? I would remember to ask later. Right now, I knew what he wanted, what we both wanted, and it wasn't talk. He was giving me a chance to change my mind.

"Yes," I replied in a breathy voice. I could hear the hunger in my voice and knew he heard it, too.

With his lightning fast reflexes, he swept me off the couch and carried me up the stairs to the bedroom. He cradled me against his bare chest with one strong arm while the other flung back the bedspread, exposing the crisp, white sheets.

I expected him to throw me down on the bed, but he surprised me by gently lowering me to my feet, keeping our bodies pressed together. He towered over me, at least a foot taller than my five feet, four inches. It put his chest at face level, and I ran my tongue over the nipple in front of me. He stiffened, back arching, and the tiny bud twitched. I traced my tongue to the other nipple and drew it into my mouth, scraping my teeth across the sensitive bud, running my fingers through his glorious chest hair. His hands rested lightly on my shoulders and I understood. He would cede some of his control. For now.

I unbuckled his belt, unbuttoned the jeans, and followed the trail of hair with my tongue to where it disappeared below his waistband. Dropping to my knees, I pulled down on all the clothing, and Quinn stepped out, kicking away the pile. He must have taken his shoes off at some point, because I encountered no obstacles.

When he was completely nude before me, I leaned back on my heels and admired the view. "Magnificent," I breathed before I took him in my mouth. It was a gentle taking; I wanted to taste him, to savor the unique, earthy aroma of his body. It was a scent of nature, of wild things, of power. I took just the tip, and rolled my tongue around the rim, flicking gently, tasting. Then my hand stroked the length of him while my mouth found other places to explore: the crease between his hip and his groin, the underside of his sac.

He stood with his feet apart and let me explore, let me taste him. I took his cock back into my mouth and moved slowly, sliding him between my lips. I kept the pressure firm, the suction steady, and quickened the pace. He was massive, and I couldn't come close to taking all of him that way. I circled my hand around the base of his shaft and stroked in time with my lips. His hips began to move, and he threaded his fingers into my hair, pulling me, pumping into me, letting me know it felt good.

"Sit," he murmured. It wasn't a command for me quit what I was doing. It was a plea. He needed to sit down before he fell down, and I guided him to the bed where he gratefully collapsed against the edge. I was afraid he'd stop me, and I wasn't ready—I wanted to taste more than the drops I'd had so far. I wanted all of him.

I looked up into his lust-filled face. "Watch me," I whispered.

Quinn's eyes were dark with need. "Yes," he said on a breath. He leaned back on his elbows, his rock-hard thighs on either side of my shoulders.

I took his cock into my mouth with one hard thrust, pushing it against the back of my throat. Again and again, until he began to swell even larger. I cupped his testicles in one hand and with the other began to stroke very quickly. When his balls drew up tight, I shortened my strokes and increased the suction. His sharp intake of breath let me know he was close. He was quivering with his pending release. I risked a look at his face and found him watching me, as I'd requested.

As soon as our gazes locked, he came. His seed was white-hot against the back of my throat, and I swallowed convulsively. He never looked away, never closed his eyes, and the moan of his release shivered through me. When he was spent, I gentled the pressure, and finished with licks and kisses, savoring the taste of him, capturing every drop with my tongue.

We stayed like that for a while, Quinn leaning back on the bed, my face pressed against his groin. When he finally sat up, he pulled me to him and kissed me long and hard, and I knew he could taste himself on my tongue.

"My turn," he said when he finally let me go. I knew then that he understood that what we'd just done had been as much about my pleasure as his. I'd wanted him in my mouth and I hadn't wanted to stop. Now he would bring me pleasure, and from his words and the look on his face, I knew he would enjoy it every bit as much as I would.

He brought me to my feet so that I stood in front of him, naked from the waist up. His eyes lit up at the trace of blue silk that peeked out from the waistband of my jeans. I slowly turned so he could get a better view from behind and undid the front of my jeans, pushing them partway down, revealing more of the thong. From the appreciative sound he made from deep in his chest, I guessed Quinn was a man who admired lingerie. Or maybe it was just bare ass cheeks he found so attractive.

Slipping his hands around my waist, his tongue explored my lower back, pausing to nip at the sensitive skin, pulling at the silk with his teeth. He pushed my jeans the rest of the way down and I stepped out, completely revealing my ass to him. He bit one cheek, and then the other, drawing a little yip from me at the sharp bite of pain.

Quinn turned me to face him. "Gives a whole new meaning to turning the other cheek," he said, and his voice was a deep rumble against my lower belly.

I laughed and pulled his head tight against my stomach.

Quinn slid to the floor, kneeling in front of me and turned me so that my back was to the bed. "Stay there," he ordered. "I want to look at you."

His gaze raked my body. He paused to lick or kiss at every spot that captured his attention. It took him a long time to meet my gaze. We were nearly the same height with him on his knees and me standing.

"Delicious," he said, and he raised his mouth to mine for another long, hot kiss. Then he began the return trip.

When he got to the patch of blue silk between my legs, he inhaled deeply. His finger scraped against the fabric just over my mound and I shuddered in anticipation. Quinn gave another one of his growls and pushed me back onto the bed, leaving my feet dangling over the side. He pulled the thong from my hips and pushed my knees further apart. Lowering his mouth to my thigh, he began trailing kisses up one side, coming close to my center, before switching to the other leg. It was an exquisite torture.

His mouth was hot against my skin, the shadow of his beard scraped against the tender skin of my inner thighs. The open-mouth kisses became velvet tongue as he moved to my mons. He lightly flicked at the moisture pooling between my legs. Then his mouth closed over my lower lips, and my hips bucked hard. His tongue separated the folds of my pussy, stroked me, pierced me. He grabbed my ankles, put them over his shoulders, and placed his hands under my hips. He raised me to his mouth, languidly running his tongue from front to back, intimate, intoxicating.

Quinn's tongue found my clitoris and he circled and flicked against the hard nub. My back arched, and I pushed my hips harder against his mouth. I was so close to the edge.

"Wait," I gasped. "Inside me. Want you." I was nearly incoherent with desire.

He rose to his knees and let my legs fall to his forearms. He rubbed the head of his cock in the wetness of my desire. He pushed against my swollen folds, pushed through the tightness, pushed until his cock was buried to the hilt. Slowly, he began to move. He glided back until he was nearly out, before he thrust deep and hard. I met his thrusts, lifting my hips, reveling in the perfection of his body in mine.

He was kneeling on the floor, his hips perfectly positioned, and he raised my ankles back to his shoulders. The angle he entered, on a slight upward tilt, rubbed against a spot that sent pleasure rolling in waves that connected to a small spot behind my navel and began to build. It was a pleasure that bordered on pain, on too much sensation, on an overwhelming need for release.

I dropped my feet, and Quinn smoothly pushed me farther onto the bed and covered me with his hard, hot body. His mouth found mine even as he changed the rhythm and angle yet again. Quinn surrounded me; his hair was a silky curtain, his scent an exotic mixture of earth and musk, and he filled me. *Dear God, he filled me.* The pool rippled and began to overflow, drawing from the kiss, from his fingers on my nipple, the feel of his skin against mine.

"Oh God, I can't—"

"Come for me, Katie—"

The pleasure started to spill, to push back out from the center of me, following nerve endings to every part of my body. I closed my eyes and stars exploded behind the lids, my hips bucked and my back arched. I shuddered as muscles and nerves trembled in places that had never been awakened before. Higher, harder, deeper.

I think I screamed. Neither of us went quietly. His deep, guttural voice escaped in moans and growls, in whispered soothing comments. Then my hands were at his back, pulling him close. I wanted to hide my face, hide the tears that suddenly filled my eyes and spilled into my hair.

Quinn was too perceptive, too aware. He rolled us to our sides, and with the difference in our heights, I was cocooned against his chest. His hand gently brushed a tear from my cheek, and then he cradled me tightly against his chest. He didn't ask; just let me know by that simple gesture that whatever I was feeling was all right. I couldn't have explained, even if he'd asked. I was simply overwhelmed by the beauty of the moment, the perfection of the loving.

A gentle hand stroked my hair, my back, my shoulder. I felt the kisses he pressed to my head. I took a shuddering breath and looked up into the most perfect face ever created. Of course, I'd already noticed the eyes, and, yes, I'd noticed he was an attractive man. But I'd not spent much time thinking about him as a man, only thinking of Quinn as a cop. It was as though I was seeing him properly for the first time. His proud, beautiful features. Straight nose, strong jaw, perfectly kissable lips. How had I failed to notice the beauty of the man?

"You're not so bad yourself, Katie," he said, as though reading my thoughts.

"No one's ever called me Katie before. What's your real name? What do people call you besides Quinn? And do I detect a bit of Irish? It's there sometimes in your speech."

He grinned. "Aye, there's a wee bit of Gaelic mischief in me," he said outrageously, making me laugh. His face turned more serious and he brushed his hand lightly over my skin, from my knees to my throat, causing me to shiver. "I didn't hurt you, did I?" he asked.

I realized that despite the pounding he'd given me, I wasn't sore. I felt wonderful, every inch pleasured, every inch hungry for more.

I gave a shaky laugh. "God, no." My voice was embarrassingly breathless.

Quinn gave a purely masculine smile. "Good. Turn over," he growled, and with his hands firmly on my hips, he pulled me onto my hands and knees. He slid slowly in, long and hard, and apparently inexhaustible.

*

Hours later, he carried me to the shower, and as he had between each of our bouts, he rubbed his hand across my body and asked if I was okay. I was. I shouldn't have been. I should have collapsed into a puddle of boneless flesh. I didn't know how he was still walking, let alone still hard. One look in the mirror showed he was more than ready to go again. What did that make? Six? Seven? More?

We hadn't wasted much time with small talk; I knew no more about Quinn now than when we'd started the evening. Well, that wasn't exactly true. I knew he liked being dominant. I suspected he would enjoy a little spank and tickle, maybe a little bondage, if we ever got around to it. He liked to hold my hands above my head, liked to prevent me from touching him until he wanted it.

Of course, I thought with a wince, now that I could see his back in the mirror, he might have just wanted to keep me from scratching him again. Long, angry welts crisscrossed his back and arms where my nails had dug into his flesh.

"Let me wash your back, I think I might have hurt you with my nails," I said, gently wiping with the soapy sponge. He gave a little hiss, and then arched his back harder against the sponge, as though seeking the sting. Oh yeah. This one was definitely a little rough around his edges.

He shampooed my hair. I shampooed his. He didn't complain when I spilled the crème rinse on his cock and gave it a slippery ride. We dried each other off, but only after Quinn dropped to his knees in front of me, and worshipfully licked the water from my breasts and lower, relentlessly bringing me to yet another screaming orgasm.

*

We were in opposite corners of the bedroom, me searching my closet, he searching the room for his discarded clothing, when it all came crashing down.

"Is there something you forgot to tell me?" Quinn asked, his voice low and dangerous.

My back was to him, so I didn't see what he was doing, but I heard the strange note in his voice. Gone was the low growl, the sexy lilt. This voice was colder, harder. *Shit.*

Was he expecting me to tell him I loved him? Is that what he thought I forgot to tell him? We'd had the best night of sex in my life. I think I'd told him that, in between orgasms three and four. Did he think we had more than that? For Christ's sake, he hadn't even told me his real first name when I'd asked. Did he really think I forgot to tell him I loved him?

I was working myself into a good snit. The warm, pleasurable atmosphere was shattered, replaced by something colder, something cruel. I finished pulling my shirt on before I turned to face him, needing the thin layer of cloth as a piece of armor against the icy fury I felt emanating from his corner of the room.

"I—"

"Save it Miss Carmichael. It's always a fucking scam with you, a fucking con."

He reached me in three long strides, his face twisted with rage. He grabbed both my shoulders, and I began to feel the first tendrils of fear creep up my spine. This man could break me. I reacted with a fury of my own.

"I don't know what the fuck you're talking about. Let go, you're hurting me!"

The growl returned, but it wasn't sexy, it was deadly. "You didn't complain when I hurt you last night, though, did you? You like it a little bit rough. You like to let your control slip just a little. I should have known it was all an act, just something to distract the local sheriff. Tell me, was I a good lay or am I just another mark to you?" he snarled.

I couldn't think of a single thing to say to that. Of everything that could have happened this morning, a fit of male ego wasn't on my radar. He was expecting me to tell him he was the best fuck I'd ever had. If it hadn't been for this hissy bit of temper, I might have. Except I'd been busy trying to figure out how to get him to leave, no strings attached.

My thoughts were interrupted when he held the letter up to my face, and suddenly, all the pieces fit together. He wasn't fishing for compliments or even a return invitation. He'd seen Jason's note. I'd left it on the bureau, in plain sight, because I'd not been expecting anyone in my bedroom. *Fuck*.

Chapter Eight

I sat sipping my coffee and wished I could just hook up an IV. Why waste time? The paper was on Quinn's usual table, unread. I was alone, waiting for delivery of the baked goods. I heard the kitchen door open, and knew Aaron would leave the trays on the large counter, ready for me to serve when I was ready.

Most mornings I would greet Aaron, a local high school senior who earned extra money delivering for G&O. I wasn't in the mood this morning. Today, I planned to put out the trays, an extra carafe of coffee and return to my apartment. I didn't want to see anyone.

It occurred to me that Aaron was taking longer than usual. I heard the refrigerator open, then close, water running in the sink, a clang of metal, and then the door swooshed open behind me. Gregory swept in, carrying the bagels and muffins, and set the tray on the sideboard. "Stay there, I've got it," he sang out as he returned to the kitchen. A minute later, he had the yogurt and fruit, jams, butter, and cream cheese elegantly displayed. He filled his cup, blithely informed me another batch of coffee was brewing, grabbed a muffin, and flopped down at my table.

"Aaron's on his way to Flagstaff this morning; he's visiting the campus up there. I don't know what Owen and I will do when he goes away for college. He's been—

"Holy shit, KC! What happened to you? You look like you were rode hard and are still waiting to be hung up. What did you *do* after you left our house? Are you okay?"

I smiled tiredly. "I'm okay," was all I said. I went to refill my coffee, and when I returned, Gregory was staring at me. I put a finger under his chin and gently closed his mouth.

He shook his head. "Oh no. This is too good. Spill it KC. Who's in your bed? Don't make me go down the hall and look, because you know I will. I have no shame."

"No one's in my bed." At his disbelieving look, I added, "I swear."

"KC, do not tell me no one was here. You were well and royally fucked last night. For God's sake, your hips are rolling and you practically look bowlegged. Look at your arms! And you have bite marks on your neck! Not hickeys, teeth. Someone bit you hard enough to break the skin on one of them. Goddamn, girl, you must like it rough! I hope you gave as good as you got."

The door opened and Quinn stormed in, heading straight for the coffee. He missed half a step when he saw I was sitting with someone. "Morning Gregory, Miss Carmichael." He recovered smoothly. He went straight to his usual table and buried his face in the paper.

The heat rushed up my face as I got a good look at the scratches on Quinn's arms and there seemed to be a hint of teeth on the side of his neck, too. Gregory choked on his coffee. He rose to leave, I think to give Quinn and me some privacy, but I restrained him with a hand. "Don't leave me," I hissed.

He looked from the blackness surrounding Quinn and back to me. "Hey, KC," he said casually, "Come into the kitchen. I brought you something. Remember those dishes Owen was talking about last night?" Gregory rose, taking his coffee and muffin with him, and I followed with a reluctant glance over my shoulder at Quinn. He sat staring at the paper, studiously ignoring me.

Gregory was on me as soon as the door closed behind us. "Oh My God, Oh My God! You and Quinn! I can't believe it. I have seriously fantasized about that man. Spill it. Was it good? What am I saying? Of course, it was good. Honey, you better kiss and tell, because if you don't, I'm going to ask him myself, man to man."

"Shut up Gregory. He'll never buy the man to man thing," I said with a tired smile.

Gregory grinned. "That's why you have to tell me. Seriously, as far as I know, you weren't expecting him to come over last night. What happened?"

I recognized the futility of trying to avoid his questions. With a sigh, I told him about Quinn showing up to ask about Jason, about his walk through of my apartment, and about the dead coyote on the back porch.

"Quinn was offering some comfort and one thing led to another. That's all," I finished lamely.

Gregory made the appropriate noises while I was telling the story, but when I tried to leave it at that, he glared. "Oh no you don't, girlfriend. Okay, nothing too personal." He paused for effect. *"How big is he?"*

I nearly spit my coffee. "Big enough," I answered when I could speak.

"Oh God, I just knew it. As big as he looks in those jeans?"

"Bigger."

He gave a happy sigh, and I hoped he was finished with me. He grabbed my arm as I started to turn back to the dining room. "Unh, unh. Not yet. How many times?"

"Gregory!"

"More than once?"

He kept going and my discomfort spurred him to new levels of outrageousness. He finally relented when I admitted it was more times than I could count, that Quinn had stayed all night, and that we'd not gotten any sleep. Gregory pretended to fan himself and I punched his arm.

"Okay, okay, no more intimate details. For now. But what happened? Why's Quinn so black and calling you Miss Carmichael?" He gave a quick gasp. "Are you some kind of dominatrix? Do you make him call you that? Oh God, Quinn on his knees, you in leather. I could die a happy man with that picture in my head," he said with his eyes closed, a beatific smile on his face.

"Gregory! Enough! You don't understand. Everything was fine until he was getting dressed. He found the note from Jason. He knows I was holding something back. He thinks I was running a con on him last night to keep him from being suspicious."

"Shit," he said.

"Exactly," I agreed.

****

I sat at the desk in the library, put my head on my arms and thought about all that had passed since yesterday. Joanne had said it was time I knew what I was. Amelia had said to listen to the House, listen to my heart. Well, today my heart hurt and so far, the House was mum.

I certainly hadn't expected to fall into bed with Quinn last night, but what a tumble it had been. I'd never have believed in a million years that I would take a cop to my bed. There were way too many bad memories associated with that. Horrors I'd locked away long ago. Last night had just happened. I'd needed comfort and he'd given it. I would have preferred we walked away from it and not look back, each remembering a very pleasant night and nothing more.

It hadn't exactly worked that way. By the time we'd been in the shower, I'd started thinking of excuses to keep Quinn visiting my bed, which was not good. Not good at all. He was dangerous, he was a cop, and he was someone who would always think the worst of me. He had the power to hurt me, which meant he needed to go.

This morning I'd stood facing my closet, gathering my clothes and my wits, wondering how I could tell Quinn to go. Hell, I'd actually been mentally rehearsing the 'this-can't-happen-again' speech and debating whether it might be more effective just to piss him off so he wouldn't want to come back.

As soon as I'd started thinking about lying to Quinn, the temperature in the room dropped, as though my thoughts were changing the very atmosphere in the House. Before I'd had time to process those thoughts, Quinn had found the note, had believed the worst of me. Go directly to jail, do not pass go, do not collect two hundred dollars.

By the time I'd gotten rid of Gregory, Quinn was gone and no one else had been about. I'd wanted to lie down, but I couldn't shake the feeling that there was something important I needed to do first. Something the House wanted me to do. *Disturbing.*

I rubbed my aching head. My eyes felt covered in sandpaper, my limbs heavy and awkward. Thoughts seemed to be dancing just out of my reach. I shook my head and gave my cheeks a little slap. I needed to clear this damn brain fog. Maybe if I made a list, I could remember the important things. I pulled the notepad over and dug out a pencil from the jumble in the desk drawer.

Pencil in hand, I stared at the notepad. Something about it seemed so familiar. I looked carefully at the logo, a full moon, a saguaro cactus, and a coyote. It was a typical southwestern design, just some business give-away as advertising. I yawned so hard I swear my jaws creaked. Giving my head another shake, I tried to stay focused.

Logo…I was looking at the logo. Why was it so damned familiar? There was no name, just the initials TWTW and a local phone number.

The more I tried to figure out why the logo was familiar, the more elusive it became. My limbs felt heavy, weighted by possibilities, and I realized it was more than the lack of sleep that was bearing down upon me now. I'd felt this way before, on the ship, during those times when I glimpsed someone's future. My mind and my body slowed, each beat of my heart marking time. I tried to put pencil to paper, but it felt as though I was moving through some viscous fluid.

I blinked and when my eyes opened, I watched tiny dust motes float slowly across the beams of afternoon sunlight. They moved gracefully, performing an intricate dance, exquisitely detailed and purely for my enjoyment. I turned my head slowly and a small movement caught my eye. I watched the blinds stir ever so slightly in the gentle breeze, and then I watched the breeze itself. I could see the tendrils of air caress the room, cooling the heat of my skin.

The palm in the corner of the room was leaning toward the western window. I watched in amazement as it moved in infinitesimal increments, reaching for the golden light. It leisurely opened its fronds, like eager fingers, seeking that which would make it complete.

There. I recognized it immediately. That was the thought I'd been waiting for. It moved through my mind with deliberate slowness. The questions built inside me, pulsing, pounding, filling me. *What is it that will make me complete? What is the essential part of me that is missing?*

Everything was still moving in slow motion, giving me plenty of time with each thought. Somehow, the events of the previous twenty-four hours had brought me closer to discovering the piece I hadn't even known was missing.

I'd been happy to be on my own, free from worry, no one depending on me for anything. Okay, maybe happy was a bit of an exaggeration, but at least I'd been content. Hadn't I? I just wasn't very good at building relationships and hadn't felt the lack of them. I'd thought I'd been born this way; that my unconventional upbringing had failed to teach me to make important personal connections.

All my life, I'd worn my detachment like a cloak, collar up, shoulders hunched. I'd been shielding myself against the harsh wind of loss, the chill of pain. Now I was willingly shedding that cloak, basking in the warmth of the Honey House, collecting people to care about. Since I'd been here I'd had more up close and personal moments for me than I'd ever had to process before. How had all these people come to matter to me?

I hadn't loved Jason. I hadn't even liked him very much by the time he'd died. But he'd belonged to me because he'd stayed at my House, come to us for shelter. He hadn't deserved to have his life stolen. Gregory hadn't stayed at the House, but he'd found blood here, seen death coming, even if he hadn't recognized it. He'd become someone that mattered to me, to the House. It felt as if he was mine now, too, and by extension, so was Owen.

Quinn. *God, Quinn.* It was as though he'd ridden me into submission, had lowered my defenses, taken me further than casual sex was supposed to. I didn't love him; he wasn't even my type of man. But he'd stayed with me, held me through the night, brought me out of my skin and laid me bare. He had stayed at the House last night and now, in some indefinable way, he was mine too.

What was I? What magick was expected of me? There was a fierce protectiveness growing inside of me and I knew it was part of the answer. A sense of responsibility for those to whom I gave shelter, to those called by the House. There was a slow build to a white-hot fury over the fact that someone would dare hurt one of mine.

I was surprised when I saw the muddy brown eyes staring patiently at me. *Where did they come from? Where am I?* A slow blink and I wasn't in the library anymore.

*

I knew was dreaming or I thought I was. It was like watching a television show, and I was playing the role of someone else. An actor who could feel and see, but was powerless to stop the scene that was unfolding. I was on the trail that passed behind the Honey House, and I was running. I was afraid, Christ, so very afraid. Thoughts rolled through my mind...not *my* thoughts, but still, they were in my head. *If I could only reach the door, if only KC could hear me. Someone hear me, please. I don't want to die. I didn't mean to find out. No one will believe me anyway. Full moon. Supposed to be full moon.*

Something hit me from behind, a force so powerful it knocked me off my feet. I flew through the air and landed on the trail. *Can't breathe. Move my feet, must move my feet.* The next blow came, then the next. Hot blood spilled from somewhere. I was being torn apart, eaten alive. *Can't scream, can't breathe, can't—*

*

I woke with a start, my heart pounding in my chest. I wiped a shaky hand across my forehead and it came away glistening with sweat. I grabbed the notepad to write down what I remembered of the dream and it was as though everything shifted to slow motion again. The silence was suddenly upon me, a deafening absence of noise.

I pulled the note pad closer and there was no sound as it slid across the desk, only the pounding of my own heartbeat echoing in my head. I knew I was supposed to see something. I looked carefully at the pad, and the top sheet had clear indentations from whoever had written on it last. I held the pad up and examined it in the light. I took the pencil and lightly rubbed it across the surface. I could read what had been there. *Werewolves.*

The word had been scrawled across the top of the paper so hard the impression clearly showed through to the pages below. There were more words, much lighter, as if the writer hadn't been as angry when he'd written the others. I recognized those fainter words. They were from Jason's note to me.

Sound came rushing back, and I could hear the birds outside, the wind rustling through the pinyon and juniper trees that surrounded the House. People were laughing somewhere, maybe the great room. Whatever had removed all noise from my world and put everything in slow motion had released its hold.

I picked up my cell phone with a sense of inevitability and dialed the phone number imprinted on the notepad. TWTW. I knew who I was calling even before the rich, deep voice answered the phone.

"The Way They Were Safaris. How may I help you?" he asked solicitously, pronouncing it "where." As in werewolves.

"May I help you?" he asked again.

"Oh, sorry. I was wondering about a tour for tonight. I only need one ticket."

"I'm sorry, ma'am. The last tour leaves in a few minutes and is booked solid. After that, we're closed until Friday. We don't take tours on the full moon or the two nights leading up to it. Too dangerous, you know."

He said it with just a hint of laughter in his voice, conspiratorially. As though we both knew he was teasing, but he needed to keep up the charade. I wasn't so sure he was teasing, but if he was, it was a good gimmick to keep up the illusion.

I used the same teasing note. "Please? Isn't there anything I can do to convince you? Isn't there a special price I could pay?"

"No, it's an absolute rule, ma'am. I can squeeze you in on Friday, if you only need one ticket and you don't mind joining a family of five. Would you like me to hold the ticket for you?" he asked.

I closed my eyes, let my mind flow, and reached for that place that sometimes told me things. The place that told me secrets about strangers. The man on the phone believed he was telling the truth. He wouldn't sell me a ticket for tonight. Whatever was happening out there, this man at least believed that the next three nights would be dangerous.

"Ma'am," he prompted.

"Oh, sorry. I was just looking at my calendar. I'm afraid I won't be able to stay one more night. Are you sure? Could I look around during the day tomorrow, instead?"

Warm laughter floated over the line. "I'm sure. Tonight's booked, and we're closed up tight for the next three days. I'm sorry it won't work out this time. Maybe the next time you're in the area. Just don't make it a full moon. Have a nice day," he said and ended the connection.

I wasn't so easily discouraged. I knew where I would be come this full moon.

Jason had been one of mine. I would find out what happened.

Chapter Nine

I woke at my new usual time and greeted Aaron when he delivered the breakfast trays. Gabrielle was due in today, and I planned to take advantage of her presence to do a little shopping and a little snooping. It must have been purely coincidental that most of the items on my shopping list came from businesses that Jason had visited in his research.

I heard the front door open and Quinn entered for his usual coffee and bagel. He was first on my "To Do" list for the day. So to speak. I blushed a little at the images that I conjured in my mind. I hadn't meant it that way. *Really.*

"Good morning, Quinn."

"Miss Carmichael," he said without looking up from his newspaper.

Hmm... I could stay formal. I tried again. "Sheriff, have you found anything out about Jason's murder?" I asked.

"No," Quinn said and turned the page.

He wasn't going to make this easy. I refilled my coffee, but instead of returning to my usual table, I sat at

Quinn's. When his reluctant gaze met mine, I struggled to keep my breathing even. Looking into those eyes, watching his lips curve into a cruel imitation of a smile, I felt as if I had just put myself in the cage of a very hungry tiger. Instinctively, I reached out a hand and placed it on his arm, hoping to calm the angry beast that I sensed just below the surface. I pulled my hand back immediately, as though I'd received an electric shock.

His smile was mocking. "A new game, Miss Carmichael? I confess I can't see the purpose, but maybe it's all the thrill of the hunt for you."

Stung, I fought the urge to strike back. And lost. "You know, I'm sure I didn't leave that note from Jason lying open on my bureau. Did you deliberately seduce me so you could search my place without a warrant?" I asked snottily.

Actually, this had bothered me a lot since yesterday. I had left the note on the bureau, but I was certain it had been closed, and addressed to me. Of course, I no longer had access to the note, since the sheriff had confiscated it as evidence. Just before he'd walked through the rest of my apartment looking for proof of my involvement in Jason's murder. He'd claimed he'd found evidence of a crime while in my home on unrelated business. It was hard to say which of us had been more pissed at the time.

I watched the flush creep up his neck. Seemed I'd just yanked the tiger's tail.

"Are you accusing me of abusing my office?" he asked, his voice very soft. "Need I remind you Miss

Carmichael that it was *you* who seduced me? *You* who thought to distract me from my investigation?"

With a deep breath, I fought to control my temper. After all, he had a point. I *had* kissed him first. Besides, arguing wouldn't help. Time to change strategies. Growing up with con artists makes a girl light on her feet. I rapidly shuffled through my repertoire of characters. I immediately discarded the helpless female. Quinn would never buy it. He might, however, go for contrite.

"Look, Sheriff— Quinn," I tried again. "I didn't mean to pick a fight. It's been a very long couple of days. I'm sorry. I really am. I just need to know what happened.

"Please…please, can you tell me if you have any news of Jason's murder?"

Quinn looked at me for a long time, his amazing eyes absolutely unreadable. I forced myself to endure his scrutiny without fidgeting.

When his eyes narrowed and his jaw clenched, I figured he'd decided not to tell me anything. Then with a deep sigh, he started. "Jason returned to Juniper Springs early in the afternoon of the day you saw him. I know this because he stopped in at Cozy's and had a piece of apple pie and waited for a call. As far as I can tell, he spent the rest of the afternoon in an interview with one or more unknown people at a private location.

"I retrieved his cell phone records and he called half a dozen businesses in the local area, plus a number I can't trace. It goes to a disposable phone. Assuming he brought them, his computer and cell phone were both missing from his room, but everything else seems to be accounted for. His brother is coming to claim his personal effects and take the body to back to Ohio.

"I'm still waiting to hear from his editor to see if the paper will grant me access to the unpublished articles. There seems to be some question about whether or not they received the full articles or just the proposed outlines, and if it's just notes and outlines, who actually owns the rights to the content, the family or the paper.

"The medical examiner in Phoenix said that Jason died from exsanguination. In other words, he bled to death after massive wounds of unknown origin to his torso. Do you need more gory details than that Miss Carmichael? Because there are more."

It was a very long speech for Quinn and surprisingly detailed. I didn't think I liked the idea that the notes or articles could still be floating around out there somewhere. Still, informative or not, I couldn't let him get away with talking to me that way. I must have forgotten I was supposed to be contrite.

I hardened my face. "You don't know me very well if you think a little blood and gore would deter me. Maybe you should look a little deeper into my past. What else did they find, Sheriff?" I asked coldly.

His left eyebrow rose, and he looked at me speculatively. With a nearly imperceptible shrug, he continued, "The forensic unit suspects that more than one weapon was used. He had numerous broken bones and they believe something hard and heavy was used to take him down. The weapon would have been heavier and with more surface than a baseball bat, but the deep tissue injuries are consistent with an impact injury. Not unlike what they see from a hit-and-run, except the area of damage was confined to his upper body. The second weapon cut away the evidence that would help us determine what brought him down."

"So, did more than one person kill Jason? Or one person with two weapons?" I asked.

"I don't think I like your interest in this, Miss Carmichael. You aren't officially cleared as a suspect, although I don't believe you're capable of doing quite so much damage by yourself. You aren't considering something as asinine as trying to investigate this murder yourself, are you?"

The thoughts that had sprung so unexpectedly into my head yesterday turned into words that tumbled from my mouth. "Jason sought shelter at the Honey House and that makes him my responsibility. I'll do whatever it takes to make sure his killer is caught."

I stood to leave and Quinn grabbed my wrist. His grip was painfully tight. "If you fuck with this investigation, I will personally haul your ass to jail."

I leaned into the pain. I leaned in so close our faces were practically touching. I could feel his hot breath against my lips; I remembered the taste of that mouth on mine. Someone's breath was loud in my ears, but I didn't know if it was his or mine. We stayed like that a long time, our lips a hairsbreadth apart.

While our tableau remained frozen, something inside of me began to change. It started as a bit of warmth behind my navel, like hot chocolate on a winter day, nothing more. The sensation of warmth began to grow, slowly flowing from my core outward, filling my limbs, heating me from the inside out. A distant buzzing like the sound of high voltage power lines sounded inside my head. My skin prickled, the hair rising from goose flesh, electricity snapping. I was changing, and I wasn't afraid. I let the power fill me, and when I was full, I let it spill out over Quinn.

"Fuck," he said, and quickly let go of my wrist.

****

"Susan," Quinn said with a tip of his hat. Her face lit up at Quinn's voice, until she looked up from her jewelry counter and saw the two of us standing there. Quinn had decreed I had to come with him to interview the witnesses rather than muck about on my own. I'd demurely agreed, which made him suspicious. It probably should have.

Our first stop was Elegant Rocks, Susan's upscale jewelry store right in the center of Main Street. Nothing but the best for our Susan, I thought wryly. She looked her usual elegant self, in a sleek black skirt and crisp white blouse. Her hair was in a short, blonde bob, not a strand out of place. She was tastefully decorated in silver and turquoise at her ears, throat, and wrists.

I, on the other hand, looked windswept. Quinn had picked me up on his motorcycle for our round of questioning. Jeans, boots, black leather jacket, and with my mass of black hair pulled back into a long braid, I made the perfect picture of biker babe. *Swell.*

In less than five minutes, Susan managed to tell us she and Jason had never spoken face to face, and her contribution would have only been to fill in any blanks in the town background. The warmth that spread through me earlier suddenly flared, and I listened quietly to what she was telling Quinn as she stared up at him and batted her baby blues. She was lying.

"Of course, I don't know anything about false paranormal activity, unless you count KC's fortune telling. No offense, I'm sure. I think this is all a big to do about nothing, I'm sure it will all blow over," she said airily.

"A man died, Susan," Quinn said, and there was an edge of anger in his voice.

"Oh, Susan didn't mean anything by that, did you?" I asked sweetly, putting myself between the two of them. Considering I was four inches shorter than Susan and over a foot shorter than Quinn, it wasn't exactly an impressive gesture, but I still needed something from her. That inner voice was telling me there was more here.

"Susan," I said, taking her arm and steering her away from Quinn, "Do you have crystals? Chakras?" I asked.

"Of course I do, would you like to see them?" she asked, and for the first time ever, she sounded genuinely enthusiastic about something other than Quinn.

That inner warmth flared again. "Yes, please," I said, and I made a little gesture with my hand, trying to tell Quinn without words to wait here. Susan led the way to a small back room that was black as velvet from floor to ceiling. This room didn't have the large glass display counters of the main store. There were small occasional tables topped with black velvet. Some of the tables had crystals displayed, while the others were empty, perhaps waiting for the customer to request which crystals or stones they wished to see.

"This is an amazing room, Susan. I can feel the power," I said, surprised to hear the sincerity in my own voice.

"Yes," she answered.

"What did Jason think of this room?" I asked.

"He found it amusing. He called it crackpot central," she said with a sniff. "Then he asked me a few background questions about Juniper Springs and Sedona, looked around the main store, then left."

I didn't bother to point out that she had already told us she hadn't actually seen Jason. What's a little lie during a police investigation? Apparently, Susan and I had more in common than I thought.

I walked around the space looking at her displays, the splashes of color that gleamed against their luxurious backdrops. A pale pink stone seemed to glow, drawing me in from across the room. I looked at Susan with my hand hovering. She nodded her permission for me to hold the stone.

The label identified it as rose quartz, and I could see the delicate play of light through the inner cracks and crevices. Heat flared through my hand when I picked it up. I stifled my gasp. It felt the same as the heat that flared through my hands when I was able to read into someone. The quartz was large, about the size of the palm of my hand, and not as polished as the other crystals displayed. It felt perfect to me as my fingers closed over the heat.

I didn't bother to examine my motives, I just handed Susan the money and slipped the stone in my pocket where it lay warm against my thigh. I asked a few more questions about Jason before the bell at the outer door gave a delicate tinkle, and Susan hurried out to meet her new customer. I followed close behind and noticed Quinn had positioned himself near the doorway to the backroom. Probably so he could hear what we'd been saying.

The customer was only browsing and Susan returned to us as we made our way to the door. "Really, Quinn, I don't understand why you are dragging this creature along on your investigation," Susan said, back to her catty self.

Quinn looked down at me for a moment, and I watched his face fill with anger. He'd not been happy when I'd told him he could take me along or I'd do it myself. Now I watched as something mean crawled into his eyes. "Sometimes it's nice to know where your suspects are," he said blithely.

Susan laughed.

The two of them smugly dismissing me just plain pissed me off. If I'd taken the time to think about it, I might have let the comments go, just taken the high road. Instead, I took a broad swipe at both of them, and it didn't take a word. With a bit of an exaggerated move, I tossed my braid over my shoulder exposing the bite marks and the bruising on my neck. The movement of my hand drew Susan's attention to the marks, as I knew it would.

"Whatever have you been doing, KC? You look as though you've been—"

Her eyes flicked to Quinn, probably expecting to share her snide remark with him. What she saw on his face snapped her mouth closed into a tight grimace. There was no missing the slow flush as it crawled up Quinn's neck and colored his face. She looked back and forth between us, then without another word turned on her heel and went back inside her store.

I snapped on my helmet and climbed on behind Quinn, wrapping my arms around his waist as he accelerated away from the store.

"Bitch," he muttered.

"Don't you ever forget it," I replied, and hid my smile against his back.

****

Four businesses later, we didn't know much more than Susan's little morsel. *Oh, wait.* I did know more. I knew that everyone we spoke to was lying. What I didn't know was why. Oh, yeah, and I didn't know why Quinn was pretending not to notice they were lying.

The questions the sheriff asked at each location were carefully worded. "Did you speak with Jason Brill about false paranormal activity?" he'd ask. "Of course not," they'd answer dutifully. He'd end each interview with an invitation to call him personally, if they remembered anything important later. He was effectively shutting me out, even though he made it appear I was included.

Unsurprisingly, we returned to the Honey House without any new information. Gabrielle came out as soon as we pulled up, and I wondered if she'd been watching for us.

"KC, Jason's brother is here. I gave him an upstairs room on the opposite side from Jason's. He's holding it together for now, but he's strung pretty tight. He wants to see you."

"Not until he sees me first," Quinn growled, and stomped past us to go inside.

Gabrielle watched him go, and I noticed her mouth was hanging open slightly. She turned to look at me. "Whatever have you done to Quinn, girl?"

"What do you mean?" I asked.

"He's been sheriff here for about a year, I guess, and I've never seen him so wound up. He's always been laid back, pleasant, even. He and Joanne were thick as thieves, you know?"

"Really? Now that surprises me. I thought he didn't like anything paranormal?"

"Quinn? What gave you that impression?" Gabrielle asked, looking genuinely puzzled.

"Seriously? All he's done is give me a hard time about fortune telling and running cons. And every question he asked today was about fake paranormal activities. I was under the distinct impression that he doesn't believe in anything woowoo," I said.

Gabrielle snorted. "I wouldn't be too sure about that, if I were you," she said and started for the door. "You have another visitor in the library, by the way. Edwin Merkham, Jason's editor."

"What's he want?" I asked.

Gabrielle pursed her lips, a little moue of distaste. "He says he's here to finish Jason's story for him," Gabrielle said.

"You don't like him," I stated. The tension in her body when she spoke of the editor telegraphed volumes.

Gabrielle sighed. "I don't know. Maybe it's just too much with the brother and him both here. I don't like this business. Something feels wrong and I don't just mean the murder."

Gabrielle and I looked at each other then, maybe the first good look of the day. She had dark rings under eyes that were narrowed by some other strong emotion. Fear? Did she think that Jason's killing was random and that others might be in danger? I'd never considered that before this minute. Jason's murder felt completely personal to me.

Before I could offer reassurances, I caught the movement as her gaze flicked to my neck and back to my face. It had been quick, but there was no way she'd missed seeing the bite marks. Since it was patently obvious I must have engaged in some pretty rough sex with someone, I expected questions or at least teasing, but Gabi never said a word. Lack of curiosity and failure to make yet another observation on the state of my life were very un-Gabrielle-like. Instead, she just sighed deeply, and pasted on a neutral expression. The thought entered my mind that she was resigned to whatever was happening.

"Let's catch up to Quinn," she said, and led the way upstairs.

****

I put my hand out, "I'm Katherine Carmichael. Please, call me KC. I'm so sorry for your loss, Mr. Brill."

"Thank you, and please, call me David."

David Brill looked nothing like his younger brother. Jason's hair had been auburn and cut short, David's was more brown, with longer, unruly curls. His deep brown eyes looked sad and a little tired. He was wearing a charcoal business suit that would look out of place anywhere in Juniper Springs. It just wasn't a suit type of town.

Quinn glared at me, and then continued where he'd left off before I'd interrupted. These questions seemed more "I'm-trying-to-catch-a-killer" type questions than the ones he'd been asking all day. Maybe he really was going to try to catch the murderer.

It didn't matter; David knew very little about his brother's life in Phoenix. The family was from Ohio, and he and Jason hadn't talked much except around the holidays. Nothing strained or unusual, just busy with their own lives.

He planned to stay just long enough to collect Jason's belongings before flying the body back to Ohio. His mother was gone, so it was just their dad and a half sister, who still lived at home. His voice choked a little on the last.

"I really am sorry, David," I said, feeling a little at a loss as to what to do.

He nodded and turned away.

Quinn and I exchanged looks before he said, "We'll give you some privacy. My business card is on the table by the door. Call me if you think of anything. I'll call you as soon as you can pick up your brother's belongings. It shouldn't be too long, maybe a day or two. Will you be staying here, at the Honey House?"

David turned and looked at me, and I answered before he could ask. "David, you are welcome here as long as you like. Take your time."

He nodded his thanks, and then Quinn and I turned to go.

"Would you two have dinner with me?" he blurted as we reached the door. "I'm sorry. You probably have plans. I just don't feel like being alone," he said, his expression forlorn.

Quinn answered first, "I'm sorry, I have other plans for the evening, but I'm sure Miss Carmichael would be happy to join you."

"That would be fine, David. I'll meet you downstairs, later," I said, hoping I sounded gracious. It wasn't as if I had any real choice. I couldn't leave the poor guy alone.

When Quinn was walking down the hall and we were well out of David's earshot, I hissed, "You are such a bastard."

"Don't you ever forget it," he said. I heard the smile in his voice.

Quinn always had a tat for my tit. So to speak.

Chapter Ten

The drive out to The Way They Were was longer than I expected. Of course, that might have been because the directions to the ranch were strangely difficult to find in this age of GPS and the Internet. Didn't these people know about advertising or web pages?

I'd finally found an obscure entry on a blog about werewolves from a young man who claimed to have had a real encounter on one of the were-safaris. According to S.B. of Seattle, he'd visited Juniper Springs earlier this year with the express purpose of becoming a werewolf himself. His final entry was: "Now I just have to wait for my first full moon so I can shift."

Sheesh, people were all kinds of weird, but he at least had attached a map to his post.

The afternoon sun was warm, baking the red rocks and raising the peaty smell of the junipers. It was quiet out here, with only one other vehicle in the dirt lot outside the trailer that served as an office. I don't know where they parked all the lime-green tour jeeps, but they weren't in the lot right now. I parked the House's...uhm...okay, *my* thirty-year-old pickup next to a sleek black late-model truck with tinted windows. I felt as though the whole place vibrated with power when I stepped outside my truck.

A familiar looking cowboy in faded jeans, a denim work shirt, and a cowboy hat sauntered out of the trailer and down the steps.

"Howdy, ma'am. I'm afraid I'm going to have to ask you to leave. We're closed and no one will be back until Friday. Please, just get in your truck and go now." He said all this in an exaggerated cowboy accent better suited for Oklahoma or Texas. I half expected him to spit a chaw of tobacco out for emphasis.

The cowboy raised his head to peer out from under the broad brim of the summer weight hat. "Shit, KC! What the hell are you doing here?"

"Raymond? How about I ask you the same question?" It was Gabrielle's husband, and he looked positively unhappy to see me.

"Seriously, KC, we're closed. Come back Friday and we can talk. Better yet, I'll meet you Friday morning at your place. I need to get going now. Why don't you just turn around and I'll follow you out and chain the gate."

Ignoring his suggestion, I leaned back against my truck. In case he missed the subtle detail that I wasn't going anywhere, I tucked my thumbs into the pockets of my jeans and crossed my ankles while I thought about things. I don't know what I'd expected to find out here, but it sure wasn't to find someone I knew.

Two weeks ago, I would have sworn TWTW was a gimmick. A place for tourists to spend money and have a unique and slightly scary experience. Nothing more than a southwestern version of a haunted house. I got that they closed up over the full moon to keep up the illusion that werewolves were real. The whole set up was the perfect fodder for Jason's story.

Could exposing fake were-tours really have been what Jason was talking about when he said he was going to blow the lid off something? His note sounded as though he'd changed his mind. Could he have discovered something of the paranormal experience was authentic? Was it possible that when Jason investigated TWTW he'd discovered the werewolves were real? Not a gimmick?

My brain wanted to resist such an outrageous idea. This was the stuff of Hollywood, not some small Arizona town. That now familiar sensation of warmth flared briefly in my belly. *Shit.* I lived in a real haunted house, why would it be so hard to believe werewolves existed?

Answer? It wasn't.

Jason was dead. Not just dead…murdered. If he'd discovered werewolves existed—

The dream came back to me, the one with the eyes watching Jason. Someone…something slamming into him, knocking him down. Someone…something cutting away the evidence. Evidence of what? Had a werewolf killed Jason?

"Does Quinn know you're out here?" Raymond asked, pulling his cell phone from his pocket and jerking me back to reality.

That was an unexpected response to my presence. "Quinn? Why would he care where I am? I'm just trying to find out if Jason Brill made it out here to talk with anyone, and if so, what did he want to know?" I asked.

"Come on, KC, Quinn let you ride around town with him today talking to people. I can't imagine he'd be too happy to know you'd come out here on your own. It kind of smacks of interfering in an investigation, don't you think?" he asked, dialing his cell phone as he spoke.

This wasn't going at all the way I'd expected. I listened while Raymond spoke in rapid Spanish to someone, his side of the conversation quiet and fast. I couldn't quite make out what he was saying. Something about the situation getting out of control. His expression was serious when he handed me the phone.

I took it cautiously, "Hello?" I'd expected it to be Gabrielle, but that wasn't who was on the other end.

"You have two choices," Quinn said in a voice that was scary for all the suppressed violence it carried. "Get in your truck and return home now or I will come arrest you and put you in jail for interfering in police business. There is no room for debate or discussion. Choose now, because I am already on my way. If you're still there when I arrive, you will spend the rest of the week in jail." The connection was severed.

I handed Raymond back his cell phone with as much dignity as I could muster. I was pissed that he had called Quinn, as if I was some misbehaving child and he was calling my parent.

I wasn't stupid. I would go for now, because Quinn was just enough of a jerk that he *would* put me in jail, just to prove he could. But, I wouldn't go without a parting shot.

"What are you trying to hide, Raymond? Why so worried about what I might find? I'm just looking for a little information to help comfort Jason's family. His brother is upstairs at the Honey House right now, wondering why his little brother is dead. What do I tell him?" I asked.

"I'm sorry, KC, I can't help you. Now please go."

****

Gabrielle was gone by the time I returned, which was probably a good thing because I didn't need to take my anger at her husband out on her. I checked the ledger to see if anyone was staying the night, and found only the same two names. David Brill and Edwin Merkham. *Well, shit.*

In my hurry to get to TWTW Ranch, I'd forgotten Jason's editor had been waiting in the library. It looked as though he would be staying over. The evening was going to be long enough without talking to Merkham, too. I'd rather tackle his questions in the morning, when I was fresher.

I wished I wasn't meeting David for dinner because I wanted to be done with talking for the day. I'd remembered to stop at G&O on the way home to pick up a roasted chicken. Now I heated a tray of appetizers and tossed the salad with dressing. I'd already set up for dinner in my apartment, since it was a lot more private than the large dining room.

It turned out that I didn't have to talk. David brought pictures. I just looked and listened as he remembered their childhood, their half sister, their parents, a loving home. He felt guilty at the separation of the last few years. Not one of intent, but a separation of neglect. They'd both been busy living their lives, secure in the knowledge that they would always be there for each other.

After dinner, I walked David to the door, and he thanked me for the evening. I was very glad to have brought him some comfort, but I was desperately tired and needed to be alone.

"Thank you, KC. I don't know how I would have made it through this night without you."

"My pleasure, I'll see you in the morning. There will be lots of coffee, plus a light breakfast, if you're interested."

"I could be interested in a lot more," he whispered softly, and lowered his mouth to mine.

The kiss was a brush of lips, our bodies not touching. It was a tempting offer. I felt emotionally bruised from my contact with Quinn. David was battered from the news of his brother's death. We could offer each other a gentle loving, and the comfort of another's arms. But he wasn't the man I wanted.

I kept the kiss casual and pulled my hips back from the more intimate contact. David pulled his head back, his response showed an immediate awareness that I wasn't interested in other activities.

"I'm sorry, KC."

"No need. It was a lovely thought. I'll see you in the morning, David," I said and brushed another quick kiss against his mouth.

He quirked a grin at me, so much like his brother's that it made my heart lurch a little. "You know where to find me, if you change your mind." He smiled.

I closed the door behind him. It disturbed me to realize that since I'd lived here, I'd been alone in my apartment with three different men and each of them had sexually responded to me. It wasn't a matter of false modesty. I was attractive enough to garner my share of passes, but I wasn't anywhere close to irresistible. Three for three seemed a bit much.

Shaking off my thoughts, I practically ran to my bedroom in my desire for bed, for sleep. It had been a very long day after a miserably long night. After the debacle with Quinn yesterday morning, I hadn't the heart to even go to my room last night. Instead, I'd tossed and turned on the couch, between fitful bouts of sleep.

Now, I stripped naked, pulled the crystal from my pocket, and plopped onto the bed. Suddenly, I was surrounded by the scent of Quinn, and our loving. I breathed in deeply of the musky smell. I told myself I was too tired to change the sheets. I lied.

The crystal began to heat and it was much hotter than it had been in my pocket. I was so tired I couldn't even reach the nightstand to set it down. I let the crystal slide out of my hand to land beside my pillow, closed my eyes, and I was asleep within seconds.

****

Quinn's mouth was on my breast, pulling at my nipple hard enough that it pressed against his upper palate. A straight path of desire flared from my breast to my pussy. A moan of hunger escaped my throat and my legs fell open in invitation. His tongue trailed along my ribs, across my belly, lower, reaching between my legs. Hot, wet velvet spread me open, pierced me, and lapped my flowing juices.

I threw my head back, whimpering with the pleasure and Quinn rumbled low in his throat. His tongue glided over me, spreading my moisture, and he slipped a finger inside.

"Mmmmore," I moaned, and pushed against his hand as he slipped another finger inside my pussy. He moved his mouth to my clit, and lightly flicked his tongue against the hard nub. Then as he began to thrust his fingers rhythmically, he rubbed harder with his tongue, and the edges of the world began to blur.

"Don't stop," I gasped. "So close, oh—"

The sounds of an alarm split the air just as the waves of pleasure began to reach for me, to pull me over that ledge, and give me release. I tried to make sense of it, tried to tell myself that the noise was a klaxon warning of pending orgasm. Unfortunately, my consciousness dragged me back from the edge, and left me hanging by a thread.

Damn! It was time to get up, time to see to the business of the day.

My heart was pounding and my breath sounded harsh in the early morning stillness. I moaned against the pent up desire and tried to still the nudge of anticipation that came with knowing Quinn would be downstairs in just a little while. It was a foolish and uncharacteristic thought.

I forced my fuzzy morning-brain to face reality and remembered everything I stood for. I didn't fuck men I didn't like, and I *definitely* didn't like Quinn. He was arrogant and bossy, and worst of all… he was a cop.

Then I ignored my sensibilities, closed my eyes, and conjured a picture of Quinn, hard and firm above me. I remembered his eyes sleepy with the heat of desire, his heavy testicles slapping against my skin. I slipped my hand between my legs and let the memory of Quinn finish taking me. When my release came, Quinn's name was hot against my lips.

Chapter Eleven

Quinn was drinking a cup of coffee when I raced into the dining room, a little late from my extracurricular activity.

"Thanks for making the coffee. It smells good. Just what I needed." I ventured a smile.

"Why's that?" he asked, without looking up from his paper. "Were you up late fucking David?"

I blinked. A really slow blink. The smile slipped from my face, and I felt a slow burn creep up my cheeks. He didn't even do me the courtesy of looking up when he insulted me. I swallowed a sigh. I knew what he was doing. It was another stupid cop trick to find out more information. I refused to take the bait and issue a denial.

"I *was* up late, as a matter of fact," I said. A slow smile curved my lips and my voice was morning-husky. It was up to him whether he wanted my comment to confirm or deny his supposition.

I left Quinn to wonder about my answer while I retrieved the trays of food from the kitchen. It was quick work, since the coffee was made and both of the large carafes were already in the dining room. Maybe Quinn wasn't completely useless after all. Good to know.

"Quinn, how'd you get in?" I asked, pouring myself a second cup of coffee and taking my usual seat. Every morning, we were the only two people in the dining room, and yet we never sat near each other.

"The door unlocks when I get here," he said, still looking at the paper.

"Seriously? Is that something I should get fixed? Or is that part of the magick?" Yeah, I was fishing to see just how much he knew about the House.

"Part of the magick. When Joanne was here, the door opened at five every morning. I could always hear the lock click as I walked up. Now it waits until six-thirty. If I arrive earlier, nothing happens.

I sent a silent thanks to the house and scooped out the last drop of my yogurt while I pondered my list of things to do. I needed to meet with Jason's editor, clean out Jason's room if Quinn was finished with it, and get the scoop on TWTW Ranch. Gregory and Owen were coming for dinner and a soak in the hot tub.

The hot tub made me think of Ted Sparks' new business, Rapture. I would go there this morning, I decided, as soon as I spoke with Merkham.

"Quinn?" I asked, my curiosity temporarily overruling my good sense. "What do you know about Rapture?"

"I assume you're referring to Sparks' and not something more biblical?" he said. He was such a smart ass.

"Yes, I mean the business owned by Ted Sparks. Did Jason go there?" I asked.

Quinn gave a sigh. "I can't find any proof of a visit, if he did. There's no record of phone calls and with his notes missing, no way to prove he was investigating them."

I thought about it for a minute and realized things would go a lot easier if I could keep Quinn talking to me, rather than piss him off. I decided to ask him about my idea rather than just tell him what I was going to do.

"I want to go to Rapture and look around." I put up a hand as he started to protest. "I don't mean look around like you would. I mean, look around as though I'm new in town. I own the Honey House, and I want to collect information about local attractions for my guests.

"It's a perfectly reasonable excuse for me to go there. Maybe I could meet with the manager, and have a heart-to-heart about how badly Jason's article hurt me, see if she was expecting any fallout from the series. I won't do anything stupid." Then I added, "You know I'm good at making people believe me. I won't have any problem." It came out sounding more bitter than I expected.

Quinn looked at me for a long minute. I could almost feel him weighing the advantages of having me ask questions, rather than telling me to stay the hell away from his investigation. Curiosity won out.

We discussed strategy and I promised to tell him everything as soon as I came out. I also promised not to try anything dangerous, just go in as a fellow business owner, talk for a bit, and then right back out. We were discussing how soon I should leave when a voice broke into our conversation.

"Good morning, sorry to interrupt. I'm Edwin Merkham. I am… I was Jason's editor."

"Good morning, Mr. Merkham, please come in. I'm sorry for your loss," I said. He was a big man, with salt and pepper hair, leaning to salt. He was large, but soft. Like a former athlete who no longer took time to care for himself. His pallor and black framed glasses gave the distinct impression of a man who was now more at home behind a desk than out in the real world. He looked out of place and time wearing blue jeans and a yellow polo.

Quinn surprised me by sitting back and staring at the man. No introduction, no barging into my conversation. Just stared for a minute, and then turned back to his newspaper. *Interesting.*

After Edwin filled his coffee and grabbed two muffins, we sat and began to speak of Jason. Even though Jason hadn't been with the paper long, Edwin was full of praise for Jason's future. This paranormal series would have been his big break, possibly big enough to merit his own byline. I didn't know much about newspaper publishing, but I knew enough to realize that was a big deal.

He looked nervously over at Quinn, leaned in closer, and dropped his voice even lower. "I wonder if I could see his room? To see if any of the newspaper's property is in there, I mean."

"What kind of property?" I asked, not bothering to lower my voice to match his.

"You know, computer, notebooks, research. Things like that," he said.

"I'm sorry, Mr. Merkham. The police still have the room cordoned off. I don't know when they will release it. Let's ask.

"Quinn, I don't know if you heard, but this is Mr. Edwin Merkham, from the Phoenix Chronicle. He was Jason's editor, and he'd like to see if any of the newspaper's property is in Jason's room. Do you know when you might release it?"

Merkham looked a bit panicky that I'd asked the sheriff right in front of him. With a predatory smile, Quinn delivered the bad news.

"I'm afraid if that's the only reason you came to town, you're out of luck, Merkham. Once the evidence techs finish with the scene, my office will turn over all personal effects to Mr. Brill's next of kin. You'll have to contact the family in Ohio for more information."

Well, wasn't that an interesting answer.

"Oh, yes…well thanks, I will." Merkham looked at me then, a long, searching look, before his gaze flicked to Quinn, then back to me. "I wonder if I might stay another night or two. There are a few loose ends I need to tie up so we can finish Jason's series."

"Oh, I didn't realize you were still running the articles. Did Jason finish all of it?" I asked.

"Most," he smiled, but didn't elaborate.

"Well, of course, your room is yours as long as you like. I'm sure Gabrielle went over the rules of the House when you checked in yesterday. Clean towels and linens are in the laundry room if you want more, breakfast every morning, but I clear it by nine. The dining room, great room, and library are common rooms, and your room key will give you access if the front doors are locked. Any questions?" I asked.

"No thanks, I've got it. Now if you'll excuse me, I have some errands to run this morning."

Quinn looked at me after Merkham left. "You didn't touch him," he observed. "Why is that?"

My back stiffened. "What the hell does that mean?" I asked.

He put his hands up in a conciliatory gesture. "Back down, Katie. I simply meant, every time I've seen you meet someone, you shake hands, or lay your fingers on an arm, some physical gesture or touch. You didn't touch Merkham. I was wondering if there was a reason."

Okay, that was disconcerting. He'd called me Katie and he noticed about my touch. I did touch most people. It was a sense of grounding for me, a way of connecting my space and theirs. There was no real way to explain it, except it gave me a sense of the energy floating around them. It had gotten stronger since I'd been here in Juniper Springs and I wanted to ask Amelia about it, if she returned. I'd begun to think it was a form of reading someone's aura, except I wasn't really sure what that meant.

I answered his question slowly, as I struggled to find the words to explain it. "I didn't think about not touching him, really. It's instinctual with me, to reach for people. Sometimes, there is a…barrier? A sense of wrongness or I don't know, something I don't want to get on me. I didn't want whatever I was feeling from him to touch my skin. He didn't scare me or make me want to run screaming, but no, I didn't want to touch him."

Quinn stood, then just looked at me another long moment, before he said, "Maybe you'll fit in better around here than I thought, Miss Carmichael." Then he turned and left.

Well, at least Quinn was back to being mysterious and I was back to being Miss Carmichael.

****

"How do you do, Melissa?" I said and shook the woman's hand. It was a limp, fingertips-only grip that left me wanting to wipe my hand against my skirt. I'd dressed to appear business-owner chic and lend credibility to my request.

Melissa Bowman wore white from her shoes to her turban and everywhere in between. Her make-up was applied with a practiced hand, which meant it didn't look as though she was wearing any. I think she might have been in her mid-forties, but she was so skillfully put together that it was hard to say for sure. She felt and looked like a blank slate.

"I'm not sure I understand what you're asking, KC," she said when we were seated in her office, sipping tea from paper-thin white china teacups.

"I admit, Melissa, I'm not sure myself." I frowned, as if searching for words. "I'm feeling the need to gather those of us involved in bringing the spiritually needy to the divine abundance of Juniper Springs. This is a special place…powerful. The recent newspaper article and murder…" I gave a little shudder, as if it were all too awful to contemplate. "I believe we need to work together to counteract any negative atmosphere brought by those who simply don't understand our work. We need to present a united front, to show support for each other.

"Since we've just met, and I'm new to the area, I'd like to start small. Perhaps with a mutual exchange. You could provide me with brochures that describe the services offered here at Rapture. In turn, I'd provide a brochure to each of my guests, and make them available in the library of the Honey House. I'd even be willing to offer a discount on lodging for people who travel to Juniper Springs to participate in one of your events.

"The Honey House could probably accommodate five guests at a time. I know it's not many and you primarily use one of the chain hotels available in Sedona. If you had an especially important client who would benefit from personal treatment…well, I think we could arrange whatever personal attention was necessary."

There is always a point when conning a fellow con artist when you can tell whether things will fall your way or theirs. We were at that point now, and I was very good at playing the game. It was time to do my thing.

Never ask a mark to make a big decision. The bigger the stakes, the smaller each decision needs to be. Don't believe me? Go to any car dealer and look at the most expensive vehicle on the lot. A good salesman won't ask if you want to buy the forty-thousand dollar top-of-the-line model. He'll ask if you want to take a test drive. Once your senses are full of the new car smell, he'll ask if you want it in blue or gold. Not only is it a much smaller decision, but he's given you the right answer. Because he wins no matter which color you select.

Rapture and Ted Sparks specialized in bringing the spiritually hungry to their door, and taking a great deal of money for their services before they let them go. Most of their clients would be white females, of average income and intelligence. Couples and men would come, too, but mostly lonely women. People who needed the promise of a better tomorrow, so they could get through the pain of today. They would return year after year until their cash or their credit limit ran out.

There would also be clients for whom money was never an obstacle to their quest for healing. They didn't see themselves as pathetic seekers of a better future. No, the wealthiest clients would convince themselves that the spiritual cleansing was a necessary part of their continued success and they would expect very special treatment. I was offering a unique twist. Something they hadn't tried before.

Melissa was wavering, and she was ready to go my way, but I was better at the game than she was. I wasn't ready to let her make her decision yet. I wanted her to create the plan in her mind and suggest it to me, so I changed the subject. Our Melissa was definitely a con, there was no doubt in my mind about that point. She just didn't know very much about the psychology of the cheat.

"Melissa, would you give me a tour? I'd love to be able to tell my guests what your facilities look like first hand."

"Oh," she breathed a sigh, releasing the tension that had been building within her as she'd been preparing to say yes. "Sure, come with me." She led the tour in her professionally rehearsed manner, visibly relaxing with each familiar step and memorized word.

The hot springs bubbled into what amounted to an Olympic-sized pool that cooled the natural temperature of the groundwater to a steamy one hundred degrees. The pool was no deeper than four and a half feet, with stone steps and ramps leading into the pool on all sides. The smell of sulfur was biting, but not unpleasant. There was a raised dais, at one end of the pool, like a pulpit for a Sunday service. Large speakers mounted in all four corners of the room would ensure everyone could hear Ted's message. Floor to ceiling windows provided a misty view of the stunning scenery.

When we returned to her office, I was generous with my praise. It really *was* a beautiful facility, but they were land bound by the geography of the location. There was no room for expansion here; they would always have to depend on off-site lodging for accommodations.

"Melissa, I want to thank you for your time, I'd be happy to put some brochures out, if you have any for me to take along. Let me know if there is anything I can do for you." I was preparing to leave, and I'd not asked for anything or repeated my earlier offer.

Melissa's face pinched slightly, and I knew she was worried that my offer for the special treatment of her wealthiest clients was slipping away.

"KC, I have an idea. Next month, we have one of our very *special* clients booked for a private session. It would be a much more personal experience for her if we arranged for her to stay at Honey House." Melissa floated the idea, as if it were hers.

I smiled inwardly, made the appropriate noises, and let her talk me into it. Now we were partners, she could trust me. After agreeing to meet the following week to walk through the accommodations, I once again turned to go.

"Oh, I almost forgot Melissa. I really want to apologize for any trouble that awful reporter might have caused when he visited you. I had no idea he was going to go after me so viciously. He just didn't want to listen to anything I had to say, he only wanted the story told his way. He had no interest in the truth," I said, putting the frown on my face and in my voice.

I bent to pick up my purse, not looking at her face. I didn't need to; I could hear the change in her breathing. I was suddenly sure she'd spoken to Jason.

"You know," I said in a nearly confidential whisper, as I sat back up and locked my gaze with hers. I let my eyes fill with real sadness. "A child isn't responsible for choices made by her parents. Some decisions are just out of your hands. In a lot of ways, our situations are similar. I can see that you take great personal pride in what you do here at Rapture. No matter what anyone thinks of your boss, you *are* providing true help for those who desperately need it." I laid my hand on her arm, and when she looked at my eyes, I knew she would see the unshed tears.

"What that reporter did was awful," she whispered. "He snuck in with our last group. He lied about who he was. He took pictures of people, and then promised not to publish them if they lied about what we did here. He was twisting everything, trying to ruin us. He photographed houses of some of our needier clients, and made it look as though we were stealing from them. He refused to see we were making their lives better by giving them hope. He said I would go to jail for fraud, but that he could help me if I would get him in to talk to Ted, if I would reveal our company records.

"He was going after us this week as a follow up to last weekend's story and the were-ranch next week. He planned to sneak out there for the full moon this weekend and prove it was all a hoax. He was a bastard and I'm glad he's dead," she finished indignantly.

I gasped at her cold-hearted remark, and then covered it with mock indignation. "How dare he? Who was he going after at the ranch?" I asked.

"I don't know for sure. He was meeting with the CEO after he left me. Raymond somebody. Jason called him just before he left here to say that he was on his way. He wanted me to hear, because there was a definite threat. Jason said that he'd find out who was at the top of the organization, or he would take out the underlings. He looked at me when he said underlings, really emphasized the word. He wanted to make sure I got the message."

Nothing she was saying made sense. Well, actually it made a lot of sense, except for one thing. It didn't sound like the Jason I'd known. Granted, I didn't know him well, but Jason struck me as an idealist. He'd walked out on me because he'd thought I was conning him about a fortune telling session.

"I'm sorry, Melissa. At least you should be safe from his threats now." I gave her arm a little squeeze.

With a delicate snort, Melissa gave lie to that statement. Apparently, Merkham was making very nearly the same threat.

****

With Gabrielle taking the next few days off, I would have to leave the front door unlocked during the day in case anyone wanted a room. I could feel the House, and knew it wasn't bringing any more guests in for now. I left a "Be right back" sign taped to the antique bar that served as one of our counters, just in case. David and Edwin were our only guests, which was a good thing.

I left a message on Quinn's cell phone that I'd gotten the information he was looking for, and I would give it to him when he dropped by or in the morning. I was bone-weary and needed to be clean after talking with Melissa. I might be a better con than she was, but I felt dirty after playing her. Even if it was to help catch a murderer.

What I needed was to run, but I just wasn't up to all that time alone in my head, so I cranked up the music and did a quick set of hundreds: one hundred push-ups, one hundred sit-ups, and one hundred squat thrusts. After ten minutes of fast rope work, I was feeling almost human again. Sweaty, but human.

I stripped my clothes off where I stood and then went upstairs to take a steaming shower. I let the water wash away the dirt that filled my head after what I'd done this morning. Sure, I'd been scamming someone who was taking money from people, that wasn't what bothered me.

It pissed me off that I'd enjoyed it. I'd enjoyed seeing it play out in my head, enjoyed it when Melissa had made the move, as I knew she would. And I'd enjoyed getting the final bit of information from her about Jason, even if it had been hard to listen to.

As the last of the crème rinse washed down the drain, the bathroom door banged open with a crash.

"Katie? Are you all right?"

I opened the glass door and looked through the steam that poured out. "Quinn? What's wrong?" I asked, an edge of panic to my voice. "What's happened?"

"Fuck," Quinn said, and looked embarrassed. "I'm sorry, I'll wait for you in the living room."

I didn't hurry through the rest of my shower. I needed this time. I wrapped a giant white towel around my hair and threw on a short robe before I finally came downstairs to see what had upset Quinn.

He was staring out the back door, drinking a Corona that I had bought for my dinner tonight with the guys. I sliced a lime and got a bottle for myself.

"Do you want another beer and a slice of lime?" I asked.

He finished his bottle, followed me to the little kitchen area, and helped himself. "Sorry about that," he said and nodded toward the ceiling. I took that to mean he was sorry he'd barged into my bathroom.

"No problem," I said casually. "Mind telling me what it was about?" I asked.

With a sigh, he said, "I guess I was nervous about sending you to Rapture. I got your message, but when I got here the music was blaring, and nobody answered when I knocked. I tried your cell phone, too. When I came in and saw the clothes...I thought the worst. Sorry," he said again.

I grinned. I might not like the big sheriff, but sometimes his heart was in the right place. "You were worried about me," I said. "You of all people should know I'm not overly particular about where I take off my clothes." I grabbed a plastic bag from under the counter and retrieved the sweaty clothes from the living room floor, while Quinn struggled with how to respond to that remark.

He chose business. "I don't want to go into all the details," I started and Quinn interrupted.

"That was our deal." He started to say more, but I held him off with a hand and a warning look.

"I'll tell you, just hold on," I said. I went to my purse and retrieved the small recorder I'd worn hidden in my pocket. "It's all on here; you can take it with you and listen later. There is the start of something bigger against Sparks and Melissa if you want to pursue it. No proof of anything, yet, but I have enough rapport to roll her if you want me to," I said, and I looked away.

"What you wanted to know today was whether Jason had been there on Sunday when he came back into town, and he had. He had the article mostly written and showed it to Melissa. He was trying to roll her, too. He told her he could help if she would give up her boss; otherwise, the paper would go to print with her as the manager and responsible for the business.

"Jason had pictures of her customers, copies of receipts for how much they paid for a single Rapture cleansing, and pictures of them living in near poverty conditions. He'd interviewed some of the weakest, and it was clear they were emotional addicts of Sparks' treatments. It would have hurt Rapture a great deal if it had been published. It would hurt Sparks' current court case to have it revealed."

"You taped all that? How do you know I won't arrest you for making an illegal tape?" he asked.

"Because neither of us is stupid, Sheriff," I answered tightly. "Why the fuck do you always have to be such an ass?"

He stared at me with flat cop eyes, but said nothing.

I was suddenly so tired of him; I just wanted to be alone. "You won't arrest me because it isn't illegal for one party to tape a conversation without the other's knowledge in the state of Arizona. You won't arrest me because I haven't done a fucking illegal thing. Go listen to your tape, Sheriff. Sparks' group has a major motive to want Jason dead. Go listen. It's all on there."

I turned to walk away, and Quinn grabbed me by the arm. He twisted me around so that he was staring into my eyes, even as he towered above me. I don't know what he was looking for, but I gave him blank face back. Cops weren't the only ones with that skill mastered.

He lowered his mouth slowly, until he met my lips. His kiss was electric, searing its way through me like a storm, wild, hot, unpredictable. His hands covered my body, sliding over the silk of my robe and tangling in my wet hair. One big hand closed over my breast and a moan escaped me at the feel of all his power.

I let him kiss me, but God knows I didn't want to enjoy it. I didn't want to feel him, didn't want to lose myself. When he moved his mouth from mine to trace a tongue across the mark he'd left on my neck, I pulled back slightly. Quinn looked at me then, as if finally realizing that my hands were not trailing over his body, as his were on mine.

Our gazes locked and there was half a beat when neither of us said a thing.

"Who's running the con now?" I asked. Then I cinched the belt of my robe, and said, "Go away, Sheriff. I have a date tonight."

Chapter Twelve

My bright multi-colored skirt swirled around my ankles and a white, low cut cotton top showed off my breasts. My hair was caught up in a swirl on the back of my head, the escaped curls framed my face and brushed my neck. I looked good tonight, and I knew it. As long as you overlooked the teeth marks. At least they were fading.

Gregory swooped in through the doorway and headed straight for the kitchen carrying a large basket that trailed yummy smells. Owen had two cloth bags slung over his shoulder, and a mixed bouquet of flowers in his hand. He swept me into a hug and planted a surprisingly intimate kiss on my lips before following Gregory to the kitchen.

As soon as Gregory's arms were divested of his basket, he too turned and kissed me, not quite giving me tongue, but not exactly closed mouth either. I knew he could taste Owen's kiss on my mouth, and it gave me an unexpected thrill in the pit of my stomach. Well, well.

The evening air had turned cool, as it so often did here, and I'd started a fire in the living room and in the patio fire pit. The spicy evergreen smell of burning juniper provided a soft backdrop along with a salsa mix on the stereo.

While the men organized the food and put the flowers in a vase, I made the drinks. The ingredients for frozen margaritas went into the blender. I also put out three Coronas, three shot glasses filled with El Tesoro tequila, a plate of limes, and a bowl of course salt. I was not messing around; I wanted a fiesta tonight.

We each drank a shot, using the salt first and the lime last, just to kick things off. I rimmed the margarita glasses with salt and poured the concoction while I enjoyed my beer. I really didn't drink very often, but if I was going to drink, I usually did it up right. The bartenders on the cruise ships had found me a willing pupil. I handed out the margaritas and we all settled on the patio to watch the fire dance in the night.

"It's been a really tough week for you. How are you holding up, KC?" Owen asked, his handsome face more serious now than it had been inside.

"I'm good." I sighed, and we all heard the wistfulness in my voice.

"What's wrong, gorgeous?" Gregory asked.

I shook my head. "I don't want to talk about it; I just want to feel good tonight. No gloomy talk. You two are the happiest people I know, and I want you to share some of that happiness with me."

Gregory grinned at Owen, and then hopped up. "I'm going to put dinner in the oven; it'll be ready in twenty. How about one more margarita before dinner?"

"Sure," Owen said easily.

"Hey, did you guys remember to bring your suits? We're going in the hot tub still, aren't we?" I asked.

Gregory went inside, but Owen answered, "I'll wear a suit if you make me, but I'd rather be naked." He laughed.

"That might take a few more margaritas on my part." I laughed with him.

Gregory popped back through the door, my refilled glass in his hand. "Your wish, my command."

Dinner was fabulous. Gregory served spinach enchiladas and a fresh salad with cilantro dressing. We ate outside next to the fire, and it was one of the most enjoyable meals of my life. The company and the food were first class. Since the men brought the food, I volunteered for dishes while they went to change into their suits.

After dinner I switched to sipping the tequila straight. It was a very fine agave tequila, and even more enjoyable without all the extra flavors mixed in. I knew I needed to slow down; there was no way I could keep pace drinking with either man.

It was easy to think of Gregory as the smaller man, when looking at Owen's broad six-foot-plus frame, but truthfully, Gregory was only an inch or two shorter. Gregory had the sleek build of a runner, all lean muscles and lanky limbs. Owen was the brawn of the pair. Either way you looked at it, they both had a lot more body mass than I did. They were several glasses ahead of me and I was already very pleasantly buzzed.

I changed into what I liked to think of as my evening swimsuit, a black one piece, low cut front and back, and flattering. I brought out three large bath sheets to wrap ourselves in when we were finished.

The hot tub was actually formed from the same natural hot springs as the pool at Rapture. It was located in a very isolated area, down several steps from the patio. Some clever designer in the past had used a combination of natural rock and fiberglass to mold the tub into the side of the hill. Only accessible from the owner's apartment, it was big enough to seat six, if everyone was well behaved. I usually escaped here two or three times a week for a little nude sunbathing.

Candles glowed softly from the surrounding outcroppings, casting shadows, and making the whole area a glowing vision. Gregory sat with his back to me, chest deep in the water. Owen was facing me, but his eyes were closed, so he didn't see me approach. His hands were pressed against the edge of the tub, on either side of Gregory, and he was kissing him, long and deep, and with a lot of tongue. *What to do, what to do?*

I wanted to turn away, to give the lovers some privacy. I wanted to join them and ask to be kissed like that, too. Instead, I stared, and watched their mouths, so hungry for each other, so lost to the world. I'd never seen two men kiss before, and color me surprised. It was goddamn hot!

I finished my drink, poured another, and sat on the step, waiting for just the right moment to interrupt them. Gregory moaned and laid his head back against the deck, and Owen pressed himself closer. The kiss deepened, and I thought it looked like Owen was fucking Gregory with his tongue.

The tingling between my legs confirmed just how hot I thought this was. I couldn't look away. Owen opened his eyes, our gazes locked and he groaned, low and sexy. He gently drew back from the kiss, taking his time, finishing with licks and love bites before pulling back completely. We smiled at each other.

"Come on in, KC, we won't bite, the water's divine," Owen said. "Bring your bottle, my glass needs topping off."

I refilled all the glasses, and slid into the water on the opposite side of the hot tub. There were no lights, just the feel of either the natural stone or the smooth fiberglass, depending on where you sat. I was on a stone step, waist deep and Owen reached out and grabbed my hand. Then he hauled me across and planted me between the two of them.

"I don't think—"

"Shh," Owen said. "Don't think. No one's asking you to do anything. Just sit with us and relax."

Gregory never lifted his head from his semi-recumbent position. "God, this feels so good," he murmured, his eyes still closed. Owen sank back into the water on the other side of me, and sighed his contentment.

I felt rather foolish sitting so upright between the two men, so I slid down until the water lapped over my bare shoulders, and rested my head against the side. After a while, Gregory slipped his hand in mine, and it was a warm comfort.

We soaked like that for about ten minutes, but eventually had to sit up to let our upper bodies cool off. The natural spring was too hot to stand for any longer than that. We finished our drinks and Owen poured another round. Talk was casual, drifting from subject to subject with a lot of laughter mixed in between. Gregory was one of the funniest people I had ever met, but Owen always gave him the best set up lines. They worked together as a pair in nearly every story either one of them told.

I don't know what exactly the trigger was, but I realized Owen was staring at me, and everyone had gone very quiet. He leaned in and tasted my mouth, his lips parted, tongue insistent. He kissed me as he'd kissed Gregory earlier, deep and hot, his tongue gliding in and out, slick against mine. He kissed me breathless.

With an effort, he pulled himself back from the kiss, and leaned back against the side of the tub. "God, KC," was all he said.

Then Gregory leaned in for his own kiss and it felt completely different. Owen was smooth, like fine sipping whisky, something you savored. Gregory pushed against my tongue, pulled it back into his mouth. He nibbled my lower lip, and then sucked it into his mouth. He was hot and fast, all demands and urgent. "I can taste you on her lips," he told Owen.

Shit, I must be drunk, because it felt really good to be kissed by these two men. I needed to do something about it before things got even more out of hand.

"KC," Owen said, before I could think of what to say.

"Yes," I answered.

"You should know, Gregory and I…are drunk," he said seriously.

I laughed. "I think I figured that out."

"You should also know, we want you. We'd like to make love with you," he said softly, and he stroked my face with his fingers. Gregory slid his hand up my arm.

"I really love the two of you, but I don't think I'm ready for something like that," I said.

"It's okay," Gregory said. Then he sat up suddenly, looking very serious. "Shit, KC. We didn't scare you did we? We don't want to do anything to jeopardize our friendship."

"It's okay. I'm flattered, not upset. Now, I need to get out of here before I turn into a prune."

Gregory groaned and said, "I don't even want to think about my shriveled parts."

Owen leaned across me and planted a kiss on Gregory's mouth. "I love all the parts, shriveled or not."

I climbed out first and brought the towels to the edge of the water. When Owen stood, I realized he'd been naked the whole time. Impressively naked. *Well, what do you know, so was Gregory.*

I left them to their toweling off and stepped around the corner to slide under the cool water of the outdoor shower. The change in temperature took my breath away.

Hands joined me and I stood for a moment, glorying in the feel of Owen and Gregory all slippery and naked as they washed the minerals from my body. It was too cold to stand around, and they each soaped and rinsed quickly, too. We grabbed our towels and ran for the warm air inside.

Once inside and the laughter subsided, Owen said, "I think we might need a favor. I've had too much to drink to drive, and it's a little far to be walking tonight. Do you think we could get a room for a few hours? We'll clean it tomorrow, so you don't have to. I just need to crash for a bit."

"If you can behave yourself, you can come upstairs with me. I've got a big bed, we'll all fit. Unless you'd rather have a room, of course."

"Hot damn!" Gregory said.

I laughed. "Hands to yourself, lover boy. No hanky-panky between the two of you either."

****

I retreated to the bathroom to change into a satin camisole and shorts for sleeping, avoiding the whole nightgown issue, and brushed my teeth. I took one look at my hair and knew it was going to take forever to brush out the tangled mess. I took my brush into the room with me to free up the bathroom for the guys.

"Help yourselves, new toothbrushes are on the counter," I said and sat on the edge of the bed and began to brush. Someone had already pulled down the covers and turned off the light, so that the only spill of light was from the hallway.

I heard the deep rumble from the bathroom as they spoke, and couldn't hold back a smile. Two men! Would I ever be adventurous or drunk enough for that?

The bathroom door opened and I felt the bed sag as they climbed on behind me. "Let me do that," Gregory said, taking the brush from my hand.

I tensed, waiting for the inevitable pulls, but he was surprisingly gentle, and I told him so.

Owen's voice came from somewhere to the side of me. "He used to brush my hair for me, when it was longer. It always felt so good." His voice was a soft caress in the dark. He climbed from the bed and knelt between my legs. He took my foot in his hand and began to smooth lotion into the skin. The press of his thumbs was firm against the arch, not ticklish. He added more lotion and rubbed the other foot.

Gregory kept brushing, making small murmurs behind me. He lifted the weight of my hair and brushed from underneath in long, flowing strokes. My neck arched in pleasure. He kept brushing even once the tangles were gone. He gathered the hair in his hands and caressed it over his own skin and mine.

Owen began to spread the lotion up my calves, massaging the muscles that were still loose and warm from the hot tub. His hands were strong, and he pressed them upwards, spreading and sliding in the lotion. He looked up at Gregory then, and I could see the love in his gaze, even in the darkness. It occurred to me they were getting as much pleasure from the touch as I was.

Owen put more lotion on his hands and slid farther up, one thigh at a time, moving higher, coming closer to my core with every stroke. He rubbed the lotion away, leaving my skin tingling and other parts aching for touch.

"Owen," I said softly, and put my hands on top of his to stop the upward climb. My heart was pounding uncomfortably.

"Mmm?" His grey eyes filled with heat, lightening as he looked up at me.

"I think we've all had too much to drink. This isn't a good idea. Please, let's just go to sleep."

Gregory stopped brushing and Owen blinked up at me, his face slack with desire. He blinked a few more times, then a great shudder passed through him. Owen rocked back on his heels and gave a long look over my shoulder at Gregory.

"Fuck," Owen breathed out. "You're right. I'm sorry, KC," he said. He gave his head a shake as if to clear his thoughts, then moaned a little as he stood. He walked around to the other side of the bed and climbed in. Without another word, Owen wrapped himself around Gregory, keeping as much distance as possible between their side of the bed and mine. There is a lot of room in a king-sized bed, I mused, as I pulled the sheet over my shoulders.

Much, much later, I lay awake wondering what in the hell was happening. I might not be ready for the whole ménage a trois scene, but I wasn't blind to the desire that flared between all of us tonight. I didn't think it was only the alcohol.

Gregory and Owen were my friends. Sure, we flirted, but it was a safe type of flirting. The type that's fun, makes you feel good and you know is not leading anywhere. The three of us were comfortable together. At least we had been before tonight.

Why were the men in my life suddenly finding me so attractive? I thought about that for a minute. Was it something to do with the Honey House? There was something there…something about that idea… No, it wasn't the House but it was *something* associated with my place.

I stole a glance at the blue numbers on the bedside table. There were still three hours left of my night. I needed to use them to try to get *some* rest. I plumped the pillow and nestled down, determined to push everything else from my thoughts for the rest of the night. Exhaustion and too much alcohol dragged me under. I only woke once, to a gentle rocking that reminded me of nights at sea.

Chapter Thirteen

Breakfast came early the next morning, but for a change, I didn't resent it. I was humming softly as I poured my coffee and set out the trays of food. Just like clockwork, Quinn showed up for his coffee and paper, with his usual, "Miss Carmichael." I ignored him as well as anyone could ignore six and a half feet of brooding male.

Updating my perpetual list of things to do, I crossed off yesterday's accomplishments and noticed two items continued to languish. I still needed to find Joanne's Book of Shadows, and I wanted to learn more about TWTW.

Tonight was the full moon, and Raymond had made a show of the ranch closing for the event. I wonder if they really closed, or if it was some sort of marketing propaganda. I would tackle the ranch tonight then, and tomorrow I would look for Joanne's book. I considered if there was anything else I needed to add to the list, and with a smile wrote wash sheets. Gabrielle was still off work, so I needed to stay fairly close to the Honey House, just in case any new guests arrived.

I looked up, startled to find Quinn staring at me.

"Need something, Sheriff?" I asked. I hadn't forgotten his arrogant attempt to kiss me into cooperating with him yesterday.

"Sorry, I wanted to thank you for the tape yesterday at Rapture. And I wanted to know what the hell took you so long to get around to asking the questions about Jason?"

"What do you think, Sheriff? That you could have walked in and just asked her if Jason dropped by?" I asked, sarcasm dripping. I'd spent two hours yesterday getting him good information, and he'd been nothing but an ass to me ever since.

He smiled then, nearly taking my breath away with the wonder of it. "Actually, I know I couldn't have, because I tried. Melissa denied ever speaking to Jason. So, if I didn't say so properly before, thank you."

I blinked. What was he up to now? "Do you expect me to try the same thing on Raymond?" I asked suspiciously.

Quinn stiffened. "Raymond isn't a problem. You should already know that from working with Gabrielle every day. Besides, the were-ranch is shut down for the next two days. You stay away from there or—"

"Yeah, yeah, I know. You'll throw my ass in jail. It's getting old, Sheriff," I said.

"Morning, KC, Quinn," Gregory called, passing through the dining room on his way to the kitchen.

Quinn grinned at me. "Did you two have a sleep over? Did he and lover boy break up?"

I raised an eyebrow, but didn't answer, because at that moment, the lover boy in question shuffled into the room, barefoot, bare-chested, and sleep tousled.

Owen poured himself a cup of coffee, brushed a kiss against my cheek, and said, "Good morning, beautiful. I'm going to get my shower, now. Care to join me?" He carefully kept his back to Quinn and winked. I nearly choked with suppressed laughter. He was baiting the tiger.

"Not this morning, Owen," I said. "I've got a meeting."

"Who's minding the store this morning?" Quinn asked sharply.

Owen had already been heading back toward my apartment to take his shower, but now he turned to face Quinn, his expression impassive. "Full moon, Quinn. We follow the town rules. We only do our regular deliveries, and Aaron takes care of those. We're closed until tomorrow, like good little citizens."

"Wait a minute," I said, looking between the two men. "Okay, is this some big secret everyone in town knows but me?"

"No," Quinn said.

"Pretty much," Owen said.

I looked from one to the other and waited, and it should have been as easy as it sounds. It wasn't. Quinn was a couple of inches taller, but Owen was just as broad, and both men radiated power. Keeping his eyes locked on Quinn, Owen took a step back so that he was now in front of me, face-to-face with the other man.

"Go see if you can help Gregory, would you, KC? I'm sorry to ask you to step out, but I really do need to speak with Quinn in private. It'll only take a minute," Owen said.

I stared at the naked expanse of Owen's back now blocking my view of the room and Quinn. Suddenly I *did* want to go talk to Gregory. I pushed through the door to the kitchen just as Gregory was pouring eggs into the skillet.

Gregory looked up in surprise. "KC? Everything all right?"

I blinked, not quite sure why I'd thought it was such a good idea to come in the kitchen. "Owen is out there," I said, as though that explained anything.

"Oh shit. Is Quinn still here?" he asked, swirling the pan to spread the eggs.

"Yep," I said. Then I realized that somehow one of them had made me want to leave the room. "Goddammit!" I turned right back around and slammed my way through the swinging door to the dining room, determined not to be shut out of their conversation. Especially not in my own place. The two men stood facing each other, still as statues, mirror images.

I moved to stand next to the two men and interrupted their testosterone laden staring contest. "Why does the store close, why does the ranch close? What aren't you telling me?" I asked looking back and forth between them.

Owen inhaled, as if he was going to speak, but Quinn cut him off. "Shut the fuck up, Owen. This is my responsibility." Quinn turned to face me. "You're right, it has something to do with the town's reputation. Too many things had a habit of going wrong under the full moon.

"The short version is that we couldn't deal with all of it. We get overrun by tourists, by all manner of people who were buying the whole werewolf myth. There are other stories, too. Stories about vampires and fairies, but they never seemed to matter as much. It's always the full moon that brings out the worst of it.

"Either we needed to bring in extra law enforcement or shut everything down. We chose to shut everything down. It serves as an effective advertisement for businesses such as the were-ranch. We've gradually let it be known that Juniper Springs is a place so magickal that no outsiders are allowed on the full moon."

Owen snorted as he stepped sideways to slide around behind me. He put his hands on my shoulders, and I leaned into him, gathering strength I hadn't realized I needed. He looked at Quinn, and the power emanating from him was palpable. *Did Owen have some magick?*

My mind had drifted, and I missed some of what Owen was telling Quinn. When I tuned back in, Owen was saying, "Your choices have made you responsible for her safety, Quinn. KC, sweetheart, I'm going to go get that shower now. Will you be all right?"

I nodded, simultaneously touched that he was so protective and pissed he thought I needed protecting.

When Owen left, I looked at Quinn. "What exactly does that mean? What choices did you make?"

"Who the hell knows? What the fuck are you doing mixed up with someone like him?"

"Like him? That's funny. I was just thinking how similar the two of you are. Except for the part about you being an asshole, that is."

"Hilarious, Miss Carmichael. Now, I need to go, and the only thing you need to do is stay home until tomorrow. It's expected that you support the full moon ban on activity now that you are a full member of our business community. Joanne did, so I assumed you knew. Everyone stays inside and none of the businesses are open. It's only effective as long as everyone follows the rules, and everybody profits from it in the end."

"Is this all part of the big hoax Jason was about to expose? Jesus. I can't believe you had the nerve to call *me* a con artist. This whole town had motive to kill Jason. Get out, Sheriff."

Quinn hesitated for a moment, as if there was more he wanted to say. He shook his head at whatever thought had entered his mind, turned, and left.

My body wasn't big enough to contain the anger coursing through it. I sat abruptly and gripped my coffee mug. There were too many loose ends, too many seemingly unrelated pieces, too many connections between everyone. Was someone directing it all behind the scenes? Or had I just seen life as a giant con for so long that I'd quit believing in coincidence? I'd lost track of the game.

There was definitely something off between Owen and Quinn, something I hadn't picked up on at the dinner party. Watching the two of them in the same room had been like watching two lions circling, sizing each other up, and looking for weaknesses in the other's defense. They were sleek and muscular, and aware of everything around them. With a jolt, I realized they thought I was the prey. It was time to remedy that. Everyone knows the females are the true hunters of the pride.

****

David sat on the foot of the barely mussed bed, and clutched a pillow to his stomach.

"Thanks for coming in here with me, KC. I don't know if I could have done it alone," David said.

"I'm sorry, David. I'm really sorry for your loss." The finality and the emptiness of Jason's room made my throat tight. "Why don't you just sit there and I'll get Jason's things." I gathered the shaving kit from the bathroom and walked around the room looking for any other personal items. Other than the clothes he'd worn when he'd arrived, there wasn't anything else to gather. He hadn't been here long before he'd died. I folded the clothes and placed them in the travel bag. As soon as I touched the zipper, I knew there was more than what we were seeing. Apparently my psychic abilities were spreading to inanimate objects, now.

The crime techs had searched the room and released it, yet I could sense something every time I touched Jason's bag. I looked at David, but he was lost in his grief. Running my hands over the outside of the bag, I found a hot spot, a place that triggered the warmth in my hands. There was a small cut in the lining of Jason's bag secured with a thin strip of Velcro. I carefully pulled it open and removed the sheaf of papers hidden inside.

Muttering at Satan to get thee behind me, I handed the papers to David. "I found these in Jason's bag. I don't think the sheriff knows about them."

David glanced down and saw his brother's neat handwriting then turned his gaze on me. "I can't look at them, KC. I don't want to know."

"They should probably go to Quinn, David. Edwin Merkham will also want them if he thinks they're notes for the article."

"You keep it. You can tell either one you want, or tell no one. I don't care. Just make sure it isn't something to embarrass Jason's memory. I need to go, the cof—"

He swallowed, and then tried again, "Jason's coffin will be delivered to the airport this afternoon. We're going home."

****

"If you're going, I'm going with you, but I'm not sure it's a good idea," I said. Okay, so I might be lying, but Merkham didn't need to know that.

I'd been in the dining room having a late afternoon cup of coffee and wondering what to do next. Yesterday, I'd been ready to believe in werewolves but this morning Quinn made it sound like a big hoax. Where was the truth? If werewolves existed my plan for going to the ranch tonight seemed pretty stupid. On the other hand, I didn't appreciate getting pulled in to the hoax if everyone in town was lying.

I'd just about made my mind up to stay home when Edwin came out of his room, moving quickly toward the door. It was the dark clothes and cameras that tipped me off. He was going to explore Juniper Springs and TWTW Ranch. Without Jason's notes, he needed to investigate the story himself, he'd said. He was confident the next article had been about the werewolves. Since I was also interested in knowing more, I invited myself along.

****

The ride had been rather contentious, to say the least. Merkham was pissed that I'd allowed David to take his brother's belongings without giving him a chance to look through them.

"You really expected me to tell David that you had a right to look through Jason's room before he left to fly home with his brother's body?" I asked.

"It may sound harsh, KC, but Jason's work belonged to the Chronicle. We were paying for his time. Anything he developed in preparing this story is ours, it doesn't belong to his family. I don't know everything he found out, but I do know some of it because as his editor, we spoke daily. Now it's up to me to find out the truth behind this story.

"What about you? As long as I'm writing this story from scratch, do you want to explain your side of the fraud conviction? It would be an exclusive, I could make sure you came across as sympathetic."

"Is that what you're going to do for Melissa at Rapture? Make her look sympathetic?" I asked, my voice dripping with sarcasm.

"Oh, so you spoke with her. Well, yes, I can make her out to be another victim if she comes across with the goods on her boss. I think we could make it a compelling story. It would explain how Sparks used her, convinced her that salvation depended on her helping him. If she doesn't explain it, I have no choice but to tell the public about the exorbitant fees she's charging and funneling directly back to Sparks. I'm giving her the opportunity to save herself," he said.

"Is that what you call it?" I had to work hard at keeping my voice neutral.

"Same with you, KC. I did some background based on what Jason had already dug up. I know those were your foster parents who were convicted for fraud. I don't know if Jason's research went that far back. He should have. We could create a lot of sympathy for your story. How old were you when you first realized your foster parents were committing fraud?" he asked, acting as if he was a professional journalist instead of just another blackmailer.

"Not going there, Edwin. Your paper's done enough for me already, thanks," I said dryly.

Shrugging his wide shoulders, Edwin got out of the car.

I blinked, trying to get my bearings. I hadn't even realized he'd stopped the car, yet here we were, already at the outskirts of the ranch. I scrambled out after him. "Wait, where are you going?" I asked. "It'll be dark soon, do you have flashlights? How will you find your way back to your car?"

"I told you I was going to look around out here. This place is closed up for the full moon, so there's no better time to dig around out here without getting caught. The office is about a mile, straight through those trees and that's where I'm headed. Pictures of the alleged werewolf headquarters on the full moon ought to make good press, don't you think?" Edwin asked.

I was beginning to think this wasn't a very good idea. There was a weird energy out here, a low thrumming that pushed up from the ground and set my nerves on edge. I was starting to feel sick to my stomach and a little headachy, as though I was coming down with the flu. *Maybe I should wait in the car.*

While I was busy wondering what Edwin thought he was out here proving, he did the completely unexpected. He reached into his jacket pocket, pulled out a twenty-two caliber Colt, and pointed it straight at my heart.

Chapter Fourteen

"I'm going to go into the ranch, and now you're coming with me. You insisted that you wanted to ride along. Well, now you need to stay where I can keep an eye on you. I'm going to find the same proof Jason found and more. I'm not going to let you run off to get your little friends to stop me."

I pushed passed the nausea and grabbed my cell phone. "I'm coming, but let me cancel my date."

"Put your phone down," he said.

I laughed. "What the hell are you going to do with that, Edwin? You're not going to shoot me!"

Still smiling, and with a laugh in my voice, I said, "I *want* to stay. I'll help. Give me a sec, because if I don't cancel this date, all your plans will be for shit." I turned my back on him without waiting for an answer. My heart was doing a nice little pitter-patter in my chest, not at all happy to have a gun pointed at my back.

The whiskey-rich voice answered with not much more than a grunt.

I made my voice honey sweet, layered with a bit of feeble. "Quinn, honey? It's me, Katie. Damn, you're not there." Quinn's breathing was quiet, but I felt him straining to catch the meaning behind my words. "I hate leaving a message, but it can't be helped. I'm afraid I have to cancel our date tonight. I'm not feeling very well, so I think I'll just go to bed early. Don't bother calling, I'll talk to you in the morning. Good night, love you," I finished. Then I slipped my phone back in my pocket without ending the call.

"So what's the plan, Edwin? Will you please put that damn gun away? Shit, where did you get it, anyway? A twenty-two isn't much good for killing anything except jackrabbits. You plan to stay out here hiding in the woods looking for werewolves all night?" I asked. With those few sentences, I gave Quinn as much information as I could about the situation. If he was still listening.

"No, we only need to stay for a few hours," he said, slipping his gun back into his pocket.

He seemed nervous about the gun, and I suspected it was a new purchase. I wondered if he even knew how to set the safety, and indulged in a minor fantasy that involved Edwin shooting his own dick off.

"All I expect to be able to do tonight is get some full moon footage. Tomorrow, I'll pull their business records and track down the CEO. He avoided my calls all day today on the pretense of the office being closed for the full moon."

His breathing was labored as we hiked over the uneven terrain. Maybe if I picked up the pace some, he would pass out by the time we reached the office. Since I was now in the lead, I made the route a bit more circuitous than necessary. If there was a hard way, we took it.

The more he talked, the more out of breath he got, and the less likely he'd be to hear an approaching car. *Say, perhaps the sheriff's car?*

Of course, there was a downside. I couldn't hear anything, either, except his voice and breathing. If something was following us with bad intent, we'd be dead before we heard it.

"What do you know about Raymond?" I asked, throwing auditory caution to the wind.

"No such person," Edwin panted. "There are plenty of men named Raymond Martinez in Arizona, but none of them live here or match his description. I should have the results of a broader search tomorrow."

"Do you know who all the people were that Jason interviewed? I mean did he actually talk to Raymond? Or Melissa over at Rapture?" I asked, even though I already knew the answer.

He didn't say anything for a moment, just breathed harder. "Yes, both," he gasped, "and someone at Vortex Infusion, and the grocers. Not sure who else."

"Why come all the way out here? Can't you just interview everyone again?"

"Because Jason had proof. A picture is worth a thousand words and all that drivel. I came out here to get pictures and I'm not leaving without them," Merkham said. "Now shut the fuck up. You're making too damn much noise."

The trailer was up ahead, just beyond the dirt parking lot. I paused at the edge of the tree line, uncertain if it was better to stay here in the relative cover of the brush and trees or move under the dim security light of the trailer. There were no vehicles in the clearing, just the singlewide trailer that served as the office for TWTW.

When I'd come out here the other day, Raymond had headed me off before I could get inside, but I knew the typical layout well enough. There would be an open reception area with a desk and one or two small offices. Oh yeah...and a bathroom. I could really use a bathroom right about now.

Decision made, I moved quickly across the lot toward the steps of the trailer. I'd be a hell of a lot more comfortable sitting on the steps rather than leaning against a tree. Maybe in a sudden fit of chivalry Merkham would offer to break down the door so I could use the facilities. I smothered the laugh that threatened. I needed to focus.

When Edwin caught up to me, I noticed he had the gun back out, but he was so out of breath there wasn't much he could do. He bent over, put his hands on his knees, and sucked wind.

What's a girl to do under such tempting circumstances? Could it possibly be this easy? I gave a swift roundhouse kick, and Edwin went down in a pile, his gun falling harmlessly away.

I breathed a silent prayer of thanks to all the martial arts instructors who taught me useful skills along the way. I might never have joined a dojo, but between the California penal system and the cruise line, I'd spent a lot of hours perfecting my own unique brand of martial arts. I had a black belt in badass.

In short order, I retrieved his gun, searched for more weapons, and then checked his pulse. I'd just straightened up when car lights bounced into the lot and shone a spotlight on us.

Quinn stepped out of the car, his weapon drawn and pointing.

"It's okay—I've got his gun," I said, and then set the gun down on the step and moved my hands so they were clearly visible to Quinn. Most cops didn't like it when there were lose guns on a scene.

"Are you okay?" Quinn asked, his voice a little rougher than usual. I couldn't make out his face in the glare of the headlights, but he sounded strained.

"I'm fine. Can I put my hands down?" I asked.

"Come here," he growled, his voice a dark caress.

As soon as I reached Quinn, he pushed me roughly against the hood of his car. "Assume the position, I know you know it."

"What?" I managed to squeak out, just before he kicked my feet wide apart.

Quinn frisked me thoroughly and then jerked my hands behind my back. He chinked the handcuffs in place and pushed me into the rear of his Tahoe. I sat in stunned disbelief and watched while he went to check on Edwin.

He lifted the big man as easily as if he were a doll. He strapped the still unconscious editor into the front passenger seat and we left TWTW Ranch with the lights flashing.

****

"You can go," Quinn said quietly. He wouldn't meet my eyes.

The words I'd spent the night rehearsing threatened to choke me in my effort to get them all out at once. "You goddamn prick! I was kidnapped at gunpoint and managed to call *you* for help. I disarmed and subdued the kidnapper and *I'm the one you cuff?* You arrest me and leave me alone in jail overnight? No phone call? What kind of a back ass idiot are you? I want my phone call. Shit. I need a bathroom!"

I'd been locked in a small holding cell, the type used by small towns before they transport a suspect to the county lock up. They weren't designed to keep anyone for more than two or three hours.

Quinn had steadfastly refused to speak to me last night, refused to answer any of my questions or acknowledge my insults. He'd silently removed the handcuffs, pushed me through the cell door, and left me there alone all night. No water, no bathroom, no guard.

"Bathroom's right over there." Quinn pointed. "No charges are being filed," he added softly.

I'd wanted to say so many things, but Mother Nature would have her way. When I finally emerged from the small bathroom, Quinn was gone and Owen was waiting for me.

"Owen," I choked, my throat tight with relief.

"Come on, KC, let's get you home," he said. He swung an easy arm around my shoulders and led me out the door.

I blinked into the bright sunlight of another perfect Arizona morning, feeling unsteady by the torrent of emotions raging through me. Owen listened as he drove, letting my temper roll off him. He knew I wasn't angry with him. He nodded, hmm'd, and kept both hands on the wheel as he took me to the Honey House.

He climbed out and walked me to the front door, where he planted a brotherly kiss on my cheek.

"Owen?" I asked. "Will you come inside and tell me what's going on?"

"Ahh, KC. If only I could." Owen brushed my hair back from my face. "This is between you and Quinn. I gave my word I wouldn't interfere."

"But you came to get me. How did you know?" I asked.

Owen looked at me for a long moment, as if deciding exactly what he should tell me. "I need to get back to Gregory; I left him shorthanded at the store this morning." He turned and glided toward his car. Opening the door, he paused with his hands on the roof and looked very seriously at me. "Some things are better just left alone, KC. I know that's not easy, but it's true. I'll talk with you later."

I watched him drive off and felt very alone.

David had checked out yesterday and Merkham would be long gone by now, so there was no real hurry to set out breakfast. First on my "To do" list was a long hot shower and then I would figure out my next steps.

I'd vowed to do something noble about finding Jason's killer, and I'd meant it at the time. But spending last night in jail had changed things. I'd spent six years confined by the California Youth Authority. I'd only been thirteen when I'd entered, a very young thirteen. Sure, I'd lied to help my foster parents run scams, but I was innocent in the ways of real bad people. I'd not been raised around others my age. I'd never been exposed to what teenagers could do to each other, never been exposed to the ways an adult could really hurt a child. I'd gained a lifetime of experience my first night in confinement. Experience no girl should ever have.

I was half way down the hall before I realized I wasn't alone. Quinn was sitting at his usual spot, sipping coffee and reading the paper. He raised lazy eyes to me, and quirked an eyebrow as if daring me to say something.

Arguing with Quinn was more than I had in me at the moment. I turned my back on him and continued to my apartment. His presence changed nothing. Unless it was to remind me that I didn't belong here.

Dropping my clothes to the floor, I stepped under the beating spray and let it wash over me. It was time to face the hard truth. I'd fucked up. I knew the rules, they'd been drummed into me since I was a child.

Rule number one was never leave enough rope for them to hang you. Last night I'd been in a bit of trouble.

So what? I'd handled a lot more trouble than that before. Eventually I would have gotten the opening I needed. Hell, I *did* get the opening, and I'd cleaned Merkham's clock with one swift kick. It would have been easy to leave in the bastard's car and get away. Instead, I'd called the cops just like any other mope. I'd stood there and practically begged to be arrested, given the sheriff everything he'd needed.

That was nothing compared to what I'd nearly done to rule number two. Violating rule number two was what made people victims. It was the rule that defined my life. Don't get attached, because you can't lose what you don't love.

I'd very nearly fucked up and started to care for this place, for these people. Very nearly allowed myself to believe I could have a life that was any kind of normal. Last night had been a timely reminder.

There was nothing that could redeem me in the minds of decent, upstanding citizens. I was an ex-con and the sheriff wasn't about to let me forget it. I'd spent last night alone in that cell, reliving the nightmare of my first night in the CYA and the many nights that followed. Quinn believed the world was safer protected from me.

I would always be the one he'd haul off to jail first, no questions asked. I would always be the one some enterprising young journalist could threaten to expose. I would always be an oddity to bring out at a dinner party. "KC has done so well for herself, considering her history." Leaving the Honey House and Juniper Springs in my rear view mirror was looking like my most attractive option.

I scrubbed until my skin was raw, but I couldn't wash away the ugly.

Chapter Fifteen

Bright moonlight bounced off the tops of the trees, but very little light managed to spill onto the path in front of me. Wind whispered through the trees, a chorus of spiteful voices taunting me. I quickened my pace, flinching when branches brushed against my skin, reaching for me. My breath caught in my throat. I would not panic. It was all a rumor, they weren't real. There was nothing to fear.

I was nearly there. The security light glowed pale yellow through the woods, a beacon calling to me, guiding me to the headquarters of TWTW. If I could just get to the trailer, somebody would let me in and I would be safe.

The pounding of my own heart was loud in my ears but not loud enough to drown out the sound of harsh breathing that was coming from somewhere nearby. *Oh God.* I couldn't stay calm. The chase might excite the monster behind me, but I couldn't help it. I swallowed a scream and ran.

The branches whipped at me, punishing me for my panic, scraping my skin. Small drops of blood seeped along the abrasions. I could smell the metallic copper over the scent of juniper.

Dear God, the blood, I knew it would come after the blood. I ran full out, screaming, screaming.

Just as I finally reached the edge of the clearing, the door to the trailer crashed open. "Run, KC! Come this way!" It was Raymond. Oh God, help was so close.

A growl rent the night air behind me and I ran faster. I risked a look over my shoulder. A giant gray wolf was threading through trees, gaining on me. It wasn't werewolf, just wolf, but there was no time to feel relief. I could see the fur bristling on the scruff of its neck, saliva dripping from its maw. It snarled and leapt forward, closing the distance.

"Raymond," I screamed and I turned away from the wolf, looking toward safety, toward the trailer. I looked to the man I thought was there to save me, and he was gone.

In his place was a giant black wolf.

I woke myself with a scream.

****

The cruise line had been happy to take me back. It was one of the more appealing characteristics of the job in the first place. Transients like me were always welcome. This was my third cruise in as many weeks, and I was supposed to pick up another as soon as we docked today, but I was sick. The pain and the nightmares hadn't gotten any better. In fact, they were worse.

The doctor's exam had been cursory, we'd been here before. Migraine. He gave me a shot of something and ordered me to bed. It was only a few more hours until we docked in Long Beach. I could survive until then. I wobbled my way along the deck, heading for the small elevator tucked next to the ballroom that would take me far below deck to my tiny cabin.

"KC?" a woman's familiar voice asked.

I leaned against the wall, and raised my eyes just enough to confirm my suspicions. "Amelia," I said and promptly threw up. Or I would have if there had been anything left in my stomach.

Amelia snaked a surprisingly strong arm around my waist. "Come with me, KC," she said grimly.

I tried to mumble about the direction of my cabin, but Amelia would have none of it. She half carried me to her luxury cabin and lowered me gently to the bed. All I wanted to do was to let the narcotics wash the pain away but Amelia forced me to drink a glass of water into which she'd poured a few drops from a vial.

"You sleep, KC. I can fix everything," Amelia said as she passed a damp washcloth over my face.

My eyes closed and this time the dreams stayed away while I slept.

****

The House was happy to have me home. As strange as it sounds, there was no other way to describe the atmosphere of relief that surrounded me when I went through the door. The feeling was mutual. Whatever potion Amelia had given me pushed the pain and nausea back, but they had hovered around the edges, threatening to return at any time. The minute I walked through the door, the pain receded completely. *I am home.*

Amelia followed me to my apartment without invitation and settled herself on the couch. Apparently, the hours spent together on the trip here hadn't been enough. She had more to say.

"I know you *think* you've heard me, but the pain was interfering, KC. Listen carefully, one more time. Pay attention.

"The Honey House has chosen *you.* If you try to leave permanently again, neither of you will be well. That doesn't mean you *can't* leave, but it is the *intent* of your leaving that's important. You never intended to return when you ran back to your cruise line and that is unacceptable. The Honey House must pass from one of us to another and never before the House is ready.

"It is a most powerful magick. *You* are magick, KC. It is up to you to find the source of your magick, but it's there, underneath your skin, a part of you. How can you explain the things you've seen, the glimpses of the future? How can you explain the illness that gripped you when you left the House, intending never to return?"

"I don't know," I said simply. "There are so many strange things that happen around here, and everyone in

Juniper Springs seems to know about it but me. Are there really werewolves or aren't there? What about the spiritual healing at Rapture? Or the Vortex Infusions?"

"Child, I don't know what is happening here right now, it's no longer my time. I suspect this is why you were chosen by the House. Whatever is happening, you will be strong enough to deal with it. Your powers will emerge when they are needed. You must leave yourself open to all the possibilities."

I thought about all she'd said for a minute, and then in a small voice, asked, "What about the sheriff? I can't go back to jail. I won't."

Amelia took on a grim expression. "I don't know what to make of him, it's never been an issue before, that I know of."

At my quizzical expression, Amelia continued. "I don't know his role, KC. Or if he has one. I sense…I sense he's hiding something, but prognostication and reading people is not my strength. It *is* yours, however, so if anyone knows, it should be you. Now, I need to go, will you be all right?"

"Yes, I think so. I'm just not sure what I'm supposed to do."

"Find Joanne's Book of Shadows. It will guide your study. This is a journey for you, KC. A journey to uncover your hidden magick. There are people like us that act as instruments, some carry messages, some heal, some have the power to shape the future. There are many with magick out there. Most people go through their lives thinking the world is only what they can see. We know there is so much more, just waiting to be discovered. Find your own magick, your own power, KC."

****

I woke refreshed, feeling better than I had in weeks. I'd forgotten to call Gregory to arrange for a delivery of morning goodies, so an early morning breakfast outing was on the agenda. I started the coffee and sat down in the dining room to wait for that first delicious hit of caffeine. The door to the kitchen opened and Gregory sailed through carrying a small basket and a bouquet of flowers.

"Good morning, love. Welcome home. I hope you don't mind I brought you a few treats."

"Gregory!" I hopped up and fell into his welcoming hug. "How did you know I was here? Thanks for breakfast," I said digging into the basket for a fresh muffin and yogurt.

"It's a small town, remember?" he smiled.

I grimaced. "Yes it is. What's happening, have I missed anything?"

"Nothing. Except maybe Quinn is even more of an ass than usual." Gregory laughed.

"Is that right? Maybe you should mind your own fucking business," a dark voice said as Quinn entered from the other side of the room.

I would really need to see about the House just letting Quinn in whenever he showed up.

"Oops, sounds like my cue to leave. Come to dinner on Friday, KC. We'll catch up. Bye, Quinn," Gregory said and disappeared through the kitchen door.

Silently cursing Gregory for deserting me, I kept my back to Quinn. It didn't help. I could still *feel* him. His was a large, unhappy presence pressing against me. It was like being surrounded by a twilight forest. Dark and earthy, full of mystery. I wasn't sure whether to welcome the night or run in terror. I slowly turned and found he'd moved silently to the coffee and was pouring himself a cup. Maybe he wasn't as out of sorts as I'd imagined.

"Sheriff," I said.

Looking up, he stared out of heavy lids, his honey colored eyes dark with emotion. It reminded me of our night together in bed. I didn't want to remember that night.

"You were gone a long time. Are you all right?"

"Yes." It was all the answer he deserved.

After a long pause, he said with a sigh, "Would it help if I said I was sorry?"

I blinked. There was a problem with that question. Some people might think it was an apology, but it wasn't. It was one of those nonsense phrases people say when they should apologize but don't want to.

"I don't know," I said, not giving an inch. "Why don't you try apologizing and we'll see?" I didn't put any sugar on it.

Quinn crossed the floor until he was towering over me, and that just pissed me off. If he was trying to intimidate me, he had the wrong woman. Rather than struggle to look all the way up that tall body, I sat down and casually sipped my coffee. Since I wasn't giving Quinn my eyes, he would have to sit to join me at my level if he wanted to meet my gaze. Fair's fair, after all.

Quinn pulled back a chair and sat for a good thirty seconds, hands playing idly with his coffee cup, fingers tap, tap, tapping on the rim. He said nothing, but I wasn't going to help.

"Shit, I'm no good at this," he said, and then pushed his chair back as he abruptly stood up again.

I wasn't waiting for an apology. I didn't expect one. What I did expect was a la-di-dah story about my being a known ex-con, and since Edwin Merkham was an upstanding citizen, he'd had no choice but to secure me while he got Merkham medical attention.

From a very distant part of my brain, that all made sense. I couldn't help but be hurt, though. We had made love. Or at least, we'd had sex. He ate here every day. Didn't he at least know me well enough to know I hadn't attacked Merkham without provocation? Did he really think I was devious enough to fake the phone call for help?

I watched as Quinn refilled his coffee and grabbed a muffin. I could see the muscles in the corner of his jaw bunching and the line of his jaw was tight. He was struggling with whatever it was he wanted to say.

"The werewolves are real," Quinn said without preamble.

I choked on the coffee I'd been sipping. "What did you say?" My voice pitched so high I almost didn't recognize it.

Quinn brought his coffee back to my table, hooked a foot around the chair to turn it backwards. With an easy stride, he straddled the chair and draped his arms over the back, cradling his cup loosely in his hands. "It's what everybody in Juniper Springs knows and you don't. The werewolves are real. Jason Brill discovered the truth and was about to publish it. Somebody killed him to keep it secret. At least that's the theory I'm working on." Now that he'd started talking, Quinn looked grimly determined to see it through to the end.

"The rumors about Juniper Springs started years ago, and at first it seemed like a good idea to encourage the gossip. In an effort to make it seem more like a joke, Raymond and some others started The Way They Were. TWTW would take them out in the jeeps at night and the real weres would let them catch glimpses, but nothing too obvious. Nobody really believed. It was like going on a photo safari for Big Foot or the Loch Ness monster.

"Then paranormal adventure seeking became a big thing, business built up all around town and in Sedona. Some of the tourists started getting a little bold, wandering out near the ranch on full moons. Last summer, one teenager jumped off the jeep tour he was on and hid out there because he wanted to be turned into a werewolf. That was too dangerous.

"We instituted the full moon curfew, but made it seem more as if it were part of the joke. Only the folks in town knew it wasn't a myth, and that it could be dangerous for people to be out on the full moon. Generally speaking, most shape shifters aren't dangerous. But if someone is new to shifting, the full moon can make them unpredictable, so we keep everyone in and give the shifters the night."

"Generally speaking," I repeated blankly.

I fingered the healed bite marks Quinn had left on my neck. "How does someone really become a werewolf?" I asked, struggling to keep the fear at bay.

"You get infected with the lycanthropy virus," he answered, all matter-of-fact now that he'd spilled his big secret.

Duh. "And how exactly does one catch the lycanthropy virus?" I asked, a sick feeling growing in the pit of my stomach.

"Through the bite or scratch of an infected lycanthrope," Quinn blithely answered.

Shit.

Chapter Sixteen

The late afternoon sunlight spilled through the windows as I climbed the rolling ladder to the top bookshelf. I was determined to either find Joanne's Book of Shadows, or eliminate the library as a possible hiding place. It was now the second day of my search and I was officially frustrated.

While I'd searched for the book, Gabrielle supervised a major spring cleaning for the Honey House. From my precarious perch on the top rung of the ladder, I looked around the library, admiring the gleaming wood floors, the sparkling windows. The whole place felt fresh, clean, and happy to have me home. Maybe I'd ask the cleaning crew to come in and clean regularly. I really enjoyed a clean house, but that didn't mean I liked cleaning.

It had seemed the like a good idea to start my search in the library—that whole hide in plain sight type of theory. I was seriously second guessing myself now that I'd been through nearly every book. It was looking as though Joanne hid her book somewhere else, probably in her own personal space.

The elusive Book of Shadows was on the very top of the last shelf, hidden between the covers of a classic version of Lewis Carroll's *Through the Looking Glass*. I was right with the first guess, I thought with a grin. I randomly grabbed four other books from the shelves for camouflage.

The cleaning crew left and I locked up the front door, telling the House in a stern voice to keep it locked until morning. *Sheesh...talking to my house. Maybe I should get a cat.* No one thought it was strange when people talked to pets, right?

The place had been empty since I'd returned from my self-imposed exile. Other than Gregory and Gabi, I'd seen no one since Quinn had left two mornings ago. I told myself that was a good thing, since I'd needed the time to process everything he'd told me. *Werewolves were real.* It was nice to have that finally confirmed.

Considering that I'd already accepted that psychics and witches could be real, it wasn't very hard to add werewolves to the list of things in which I believed. Of course, werewolves scared me and witches didn't, but maybe that was because I was afraid of the healed bite marks on my neck?

I hadn't the courage to ask Quinn if he was a werewolf and if I was now infected with lycanthropy. I suppose I'd know for sure in a little more than a week. I would certainly have my answer if I turned furry.

I stacked the books from the library on my bedside table. My bedtime story promised to be interesting. As much as I wanted to sit and read, it was time to get ready to go to Owen and Gregory's house for dinner. If everyone in the community was in on this werewolf secret, then it was time to start collecting answers from people besides Quinn.

****

Owen answered the door, looking even more deliciously handsome than usual. His clear, gray eyes swept appreciatively over me from top to bottom and back, before his gaze settled on my face. We just stared at each other for a long minute before he pulled me close against his broad chest and wrapped his strong arms around me. I could hear the rapid beat of his heart in time with my own speeding pulse. Was he as nervous as I was?

Owen cupped my face between his palms and lowered his mouth slowly. It was impossible to turn away from the heat in his gaze. His kiss was unexpectedly gentle, lips closed, chaste. I raised my hands to his face, mirroring the way he was holding mine. The heat began to flow between my palms, just as it did when I was receiving a vision about someone's future.

Owen pulled back. "KC, sweetheart. Don't ever leave us like that again." His thumbs caressed my cheekbones, and he looked steadily into my eyes, silently demanding my acquiescence.

I looked away, unsure of what my eyes might reveal.

"KC, you need to know some things, and not all of them are mine to tell you, but know this. You belong to this place now. You can't just walk away. I know you can feel it, and I know it must be overwhelming at times. Sweetheart, you are chock full of magick just waiting to spill over, and you need to be *here* when that happens. There are people here who will be able to help you, to keep you safe. Promise me." He used his grip on my face to force me to meet his gaze.

"KC, promise me you won't try to leave again without coming to see me first," he said.

I looked into his beautiful face; his gray eyes filled with...something. Concern? Fear? I don't know, some kind of strong emotion. I wanted to turn away, I wanted to tell him that I owed no one an explanation. I was an independent woman, a free spirit, free to follow my whims. I was beholden to no one, counted on no one, and wanted no one counting on me.

"I promise," I whispered.

"Thank God," Gregory muttered behind me, just before Owen crushed me to his chest once more.

With a promise of talk after dinner, we retreated to the back patio to enjoy grilled trout and fine wine. As before when I visited their home, they were solicitous of each other without being cloying. Owen placed his hand on Gregory's hip when he reached to grab the corkscrew. Gregory brushed Owen's arm when he passed behind him on the way to the kitchen. They found many ways to touch, seemingly without conscious effort. Other than the first kiss, both of them refrained from touching me.

After dinner, Owen insisted that we go inside to talk. He'd steered the conversation during dinner, keeping the topics casual and very generic.

"Some things are better kept from the breeze," he'd answered cryptically, when I'd asked why we didn't talk outside on the patio.

We sat in their living room. I chose a club chair in soft cordovan leather, and tucked my feet up under my legs. Gregory and Owen sat together on the leather couch, hips touching, facing me. The tension was palpable.

"What is it you want to know, KC?" Owen asked.

Hmmm… he was going to make me ask the questions. I'd hoped for full disclosure, because if I was going to ask, it meant he could hold back anything I didn't already know about. *Sigh*. I might as well start with the biggie.

"How many werewolves live in Juniper Springs?" I said without preamble.

"Jesus, KC. Use a little lubricant, why don't you?" Gregory laughed.

Owen's rich laughter joined Gregory's and I shivered beneath the wave of sexy that washed over me from the two of them.

"It's okay, G. She's earned the right to be curious. I'll answer your question, KC, but will you tell me why you ask? What's changed since you've been home?"

"Quinn told me. He said they were real, told me that the ranch was started in order to deflect attention, and that people really are safer at home on nights with the full moon." I said it all rather quickly. If Quinn had been lying…

"Ahh, I wondered if he would tell you. And did he explain why he put you in jail that night?" Owen asked softly.

"He said it was to keep me safe. That it was the one place he knew I couldn't escape and get into more trouble, like going back out to the ranch under the full moon."

Owen and Gregory gave each other a look, and it wasn't a pleased one.

"What?" I demanded.

"The werewolves *are* real, KC," Owen said. "You were in very real danger out there that night. How did Quinn find you?"

"I called him. I pretended I was breaking a date with him so Merkham wouldn't catch on. Then I left the connection on the cell phone open so Quinn could hear what we were talking about. I knew he would figure it out and hoped he would come find us."

"And when he arrived he took you to jail?" Gregory asked indignantly.

"Yes, he handcuffed me, and put me in the back of the car. He wouldn't talk to me. Not one word. Then he locked me in the holding cell and left," I answered softly, the memories of that night pushing at me.

Without warning, other memories came along, too. I was drowning in despair, the same blackness that drove me from town flooded through me now, only much, much worse. The faces of my tormentors swam before my eyes and I doubled over in pain.

Owen gasped. Standing quickly, he lifted me and brought me to sit on his lap, my head pressed against his chest. "God, KC, I can feel it. Shh, shh…" He brushed his hands along my back, over my thighs, smoothed my hair. A warmth spread through me, pushing the faces back into the shadows where I kept them.

"No more tonight, Owen," Gregory said, standing suddenly. "Something isn't right. Something is pushing the darkness."

"Yes, I can feel it too. I'm taking her home, Gregory. I need to check," Owen said.

"Should I call Quinn?" Gregory asked.

They could feel my darkness? Call Quinn? Why would he call Quinn? Their words made no sense.

"Not until I know more. I'll call him if I need him. Do you want to come?" Owen asked.

Gregory kissed the top of my head as Owen stood, cradling me in his arms. "No, I can't do what you can do. I'll work what I can from here. I'll spell you in the morning."

Then Gregory rested his hand on my arm. "I'll stop by in the morning, KC, and make the coffee. You sleep in, okay? Owen's going to take care of this."

I nodded. I felt shaky, unsure of myself, a little scared. What would they do? What *could* they do? What did telling Quinn have to do with anything? I didn't know what was happening. One minute I'd been having a nice evening with friends and we were finally getting down to some serious conversation. Then the memories had come, memories of awful times, memories triggered by my one night in the holding cell.

I felt terrible, as bad as I had when Amelia had found me. Worse yet, the nightmares were hovering. The dreams of the wolves, dreams of the guards, they were just waiting for me to close my eyes. The dreams were coming for me.

Owen looked down at me and smiled gently. "Sleep now, little one, while I take you home."

****

I will not cry. The cuffs were loose upon my wrists, the orange jumpsuit ridiculously baggy, the legs rolled up to keep me from tripping. I shuffled onto the bus, eyes cast down, pretending this couldn't be happening. The guard patted my butt, and made me sit in the front. *I will not cry.*

"What's your name, little cutie?" the guard asked, his eyes fixed on my chest. His nametag said he was Officer Foster, and he was as old as my dad. *Gross.*

"Katherine," I answered. He raised his hand and brushed the tips of his fingers across my chest.

"Big name for a little girl. Guess it's time you grew up to match your name. Don't worry, little girl, I'll take care of you."

I raised my eyes to find the driver's gaze fixed on Foster's hands on my breast. Our gazes met in the rearview mirror. If I thought he would help, I was wrong. He looked away and said nothing. *I will not cry.*

When we arrived at the detention center, Officer Foster took charge of me and left the other juveniles to the remaining guards.

"Judge says we need to keep you separated from the general population. Says you're too young. I know just the place to let you grow up a bit, little girl," he said. He led the way through the deserted dining hall, our footsteps echoed against the tile and cinderblock. The smell was a mix of pine and urine and the harsh fluorescents hid nothing.

Officer Foster opened a steel door and pushed me through, before looking over his shoulder and then following behind me. We were in a short hallway with three doors on either side. "This is where we put violent offenders, little girl. Lucky for us we don't have any right now. It's just you and me, and total privacy. Don't worry, little cutie, if you treat Uncle Petey right, he'll treat you right." He smelled of cigarettes and sweat. He reached out to touch my face. *I might cry.*

"Take off your clothes, little girl. I brought you something nicer to wear. His hand reached for the zipper on the front of my jumpsuit. As he began to draw it down, I thought, "Oh, God, I don't want to be here." *I began to cry.*

Hands shook me roughly. "KC! KC! Stop it! Wake up, Goddammit!"

"Owen?" I asked, confused. *Where am I? What just happened to me?*

Owen opened the car door and raced around to my side. He wasn't particularly gentle as he scooped me from the front seat and ran for the front door of the Honey House, muttering words under his breath that I couldn't understand. As soon as we crossed the threshold, the terrible pressure in my chest eased, but Owen didn't slow down until he had me in my apartment.

Owen grabbed my face and kissed me, hard. His tongue pushed past my lips that were parted on a question, and he thrust, gliding in long searching strokes. Every few seconds he moved his mouth slightly, each kiss repositioned to give him greater access, he was making love to my mouth.

With each of his kisses, I felt a piece of myself return. It was as though the power of his touch, the strength of his kiss, was pulling me back from the edge, pushing away any lingering darkness. I began to kiss him back, to help push the nightmare away. To put the memory back in its box.

Finally, Owen let me slide to the floor, with one arm tight around my waist, the other hand still gripping my face, and the kiss began to calm. Gentle now, he traced my lips with his tongue, and then pulled my lower lip into his mouth before letting the kiss go. With a final press of his lips to my forehead, he stepped back and dropped his hand from my face.

"All better?" he asked with a wry smile.

"What the fuck just happened, Owen?" I asked, and not with a happy voice.

He raked his fingers through his hair, leaving a nice tousled look, and blew out a breath. "You've been spelled. We'll talk all about it in just a little bit, I promise, but we need to do a few things first, okay? Will you trust me, KC?"

Questions raced through my mind, all of them demanding immediate answers, but one look at Owen's serious expression, and I agreed.

"Yes, I'll trust you. I *do* trust you. What do you need me to do?" I asked. I could hear the anxiety in my voice. I would do anything to keep that particular nightmare at bay.

Owen's eyes crinkled with the return of his sexy grin, the one that quirked on the right side to show a hint of a dimple. "Get naked," he said.

Chapter Seventeen

I stood under the steaming water and Owen handed me all new bottles of shampoo, crème rinse, and a fresh bar of soap. None of my usual brands, but that couldn't be helped. I could buy more tomorrow. While I finished washing, Owen gathered all the lotions and make-up, and dumped them into a trash bag. Replacing everything was going to cost me a fortune.

When I was scrubbed and rinsed, I wrapped myself in a satin robe and stepped in to a candle-lit bedroom. *Uh oh.* The room was empty, but flickering candles were on nearly every flat surface. A light woodsy scent filled air. *Planned seduction? I hadn't seen that coming.* Then I did a double take and realized the sheets had been stripped from the bed. *Hmm…*

I wandered down the stairs and found the same woodsy scented candles scattered throughout the living room. "Owen?" I asked uncertainly.

The door to my apartment opened and Owen came in carrying a laundry basket.

"Aw, shit, KC, take off the robe," he said, already unbuttoning his shirt.

"What?" I stammered, thinking I deserved a little more romancing than a bunch of candles after the evening I'd had.

"Take off your robe and put this on." He handed me his shirt. "I don't know for sure what was used to spell you, but something that was next to your skin made you more susceptible to the effects. It could have been the laundry soap or clothes you wear every day. I'm washing your sheets, now."

I dropped the robe and pulled his shirt on. It was yards more material than I needed to cover my body.

Owen gave me his sexy grin, and stepped closer. "I could get used to seeing you like this," he said. He rolled the sleeve up to my forearm, and then did the same for the other arm. He didn't step back once he was finished, but then neither did I. With a jerk, he pulled the lapels, drawing me closer, and I saw the hunger in his eyes. I traced my finger down his chest, following the dark trail of silken hair past his belly button to where it disappeared beneath the waistband of his jeans. The moment lingered, built. We hovered, ready to fall into each other, pushing away all the concerns and fears of the night.

Owen slowly lowered his face to mine, giving me plenty of time to draw back. I raised my mouth to meet him, and still we hovered, letting the anticipation of the kiss fill us, stoke our desire.

The door burst open. "I can't see a fucking thing out there tonight. I'll have to look again in the morning."

Quinn.

He stood facing us, his mouth slightly open, his eyes wide. I swear, I could see his nostrils flare as a slow heat crept up his neck.

"Well, if that isn't a pretty picture. You call me over because there's some metaphysical emergency, and while I'm running around getting fresh shampoo and making sure the little princess here is safe, you're in here trying to get laid!"

I expected Owen would flare right back at Quinn, but he just turned that slow sexy smile on the sheriff. I turned, but Owen pulled me back against his chest, and wrapped his big arms around me. He positively thrummed with energy and he was oh-so-happy to have his hips pressed into my back.

"Come now, Quinn. The way you're acting makes it seem as if you and KC here have a relationship," Owen purred. "You didn't want her, remember? You walked away."

"Shut the fuck up. I saw her first, and if I want her, I'll take her! Come here, Katie. Now!" Quinn ordered and held out his hand.

I gasped and narrowed my eyes, but Owen gave me a little squeeze, which I took to mean he wasn't finished. I could wait a little longer before I eviscerated Quinn. If I had to. Then I would go after Owen next. The testosterone was so thick in the air you could practically cut it with a knife.

The silence lengthened, and Quinn's words seemed to echo around the room, as we each had time to play them over in our minds. Then Owen was pushing more than his erection in my back. Well-being poured from him, rolling out in waves and washing over us all. I watched as Quinn's shoulders lowered and his hands unfisted. It was only then I realized how ready to attack he'd been.

With a little shudder, Owen loosened his arms around me, but didn't let go completely. "Everybody okay?" he asked gently.

Quinn shook himself, then dry-washed his face. "Fuck."

"Yeah, I know what you mean. We really need to be careful," Owen said.

"Would somebody like to explain what the hell is going on around here?" I asked.

Owen kissed me on top of the head and led me to the middle of the couch. "Sit, I'll pour us all drinks," he said. "Quinn, sit on the couch next to KC, proximity is going to be important tonight."

"Aren't you worried about the drink?" Quinn asked, ignoring the request to sit and pacing across the far side of the room.

I wasn't sure exactly what was going on, but it seemed like a good question if we had to throw everything else out.

Owen carried over three glasses and a bottle of Macallan. "It's a contact potion we're looking for. Anything else would digest and the effects would be lost. I'm betting on her lotion. It could be the lingerie, or some other clothing worn close to the skin, but shampoo or lotion would be the easiest.

I reached for my glass, and let the amber liquid flow down my throat before I repeated my question. "Would somebody please tell me what in the hell is going on around here? I get that you think someone spelled my shampoo or something and that made me have the bad dreams. But honestly, that doesn't make any sense. Even if it was a spell, how could that really work? What happened earlier tonight was a real memory, Owen. We can't wash those away." I heard the sadness in my voice.

Owen sat down next to me on one end of the couch. He half turned, with one leg bent and pressed close enough that his knee rested against my thigh as I sat cross-legged on the couch. "Sit, Quinn," he said, and there was a touch of exasperation in his voice.

Quinn walked stiffly to the table and topped off his drink. He didn't sit.

Owen sighed, apparently deeply aggravated at Quinn's refusal to make contact with me. "It's not really a spell, KC, it's a potion enhanced and activated by a spell," he said.

"And that makes a difference because…"

"Because it means it's fucking personal," Quinn muttered.

"Exactly," Owen agreed. "First, someone has to be skilled enough to acquire or brew a fairly unusual potion. The Dark Maker potion can make the victim go insane, but it only works on someone with truly bad memories to begin with. If you use it on a happy person, or a young person without bad memories, nothing will happen, except maybe a rash will break out. Someone with a traumatic past is forced to fight against the memories to keep them from resurfacing.

"The first potion-induced nightmares are usually just a collection of disturbing images, maybe relating to current fears or worries. Similar to what many people experience when under stress. The dreams might be disturbing, but they're common enough.

"When the really bad memories kick in, it's truly terrifying. It's all the things you put in your own personal memory box and you thought you'd thrown away the key. Once those start to surface, it's usually a quick descent into madness. Many kill themselves. It's an insidious spell.

"Please don't worry, we can counter this," Owen said, passing his hand over my arm. "We can call magick. But first, we need to know what we're fighting. The spell seemed to hit you hard. What was the first dream, KC? What was the first dream you remember?"

I thought back over the last several weeks. There had been a lot of dreams. Most of the vague, dark images that left me feeling more tired than rested when I woke. Then the real nightmares began.

"It was about wolves. It was the night after I was in jail. They were chasing me, and I was running toward the trailer at the Ranch. Then Raymond was there, and then he was a wolf, too."

Owen grinned. "Your instincts are good. Or maybe I should say your psychic abilities. Anyway, tonight's dream changed. What happened?"

"I don't want to talk about it," I said flatly.

Owen stroked my hair. "I know, sweetheart, I know. I wish I could spare you. Don't you see? The dreams hold power over you because the memories are secret. They're your own personal hell and you don't want anyone else to know about it. That's part of the magick."

Owen turned his head to follow Quinn as he paced in front of the glass doors. "Goddammit, Quinn. I won't ask you again. You know what we're up against here. You need to touch her. Just brush your knee up against her."

"God, what is it with you?" I shouted. "He doesn't want to touch me. It's obvious I repulse him. I don't want him to touch me, either!" I gulped a breath. "What's happening?" I whispered.

"It's not that, KC," Quinn said quietly. "I'm sorry," he added, not really looking at anyone. He sat next to me, and turned in a similar fashion to Owen, so that his jeans-clad knee touched my thigh.

I ignored the electricity that seemed to flare between us. This was scary stuff we were talking about here, and I wasn't about to let myself get distracted.

Owen was relentless, he seemed to be able to track all the things happening better than the rest of us, because now that Quinn was touching me, he went back to digging. "Tell me about tonight's dream, sweetheart."

"Are we really pushing the dreams away if I tell you? Does it have to be both of you?" I asked. I looked at Quinn for the answer first this time. He gave one sharp nod, but he didn't look happy. Owen continued to stroke my hair.

"Let's get it over with," I said. I was glad the lights were dim and we had only the flickering candles to show my face. I looked down at my lap. I didn't want to see the pity in Owen's eyes and I thought I would scream if Quinn turned his cop eyes on me. I told them about the dream, about the memory.

Owen moved closer, silently offering comfort. Quinn stayed tightly contained, his knee just brushing my thigh. I left the memory at the first night, about Foster leading me into the isolation cells. I didn't add any more detail than that. They could use their imaginations, the rest was just more of the same. It should be more than enough for Owen and Quinn to understand the nature of my dreams and the memories.

"Is that where the dream stopped tonight, KC?" Owen asked in a just-the-facts manner.

"Yes."

"What happened next in the memory?" he asked, still matter-of-fact. "I know, sweetheart," Owen said as a shudder racked through me.

I did not want to share. Every piece of the memory was horrifying. Humiliating. *Shameful.*

Owen seemed to sense my reluctance because he offered comfort in the form of an explanation. "You need to tell us all of it, KC. We're going to become your secret keepers. Once a secret is shared, it no longer has the power to turn against you. Once you share this memory with us, no one can twist it inside you ever again. They would have to bespell all three of us, and that can't happen. I know this is hard, but you need to tell us, so we can keep you safe."

I turned my sight inward, remembering. This was not a story I ever thought I'd tell anyone. Gripping my hands tightly together, I stared into my lap. With a sigh, I started.

"There was a court appointed guardian who was supposed to check on me and make sure the judge's orders were followed. She couldn't find me. There was no official record of where they were holding me, she said I got lost in the system, somehow. It took nine weeks to locate me in the juvenile isolation unit. I was no longer the well-fed, well-groomed young girl that had been sentenced to eight years of juvenile detention.

"When she took me back before the judge, he allowed that some misuse of power *might* have occurred. Due to the circumstances, he authorized a state provided abortion, and he reduced my sentence by two years. Because of that, I was released when I turned nineteen, instead of twenty-one." I might have left out a detail or two, but that was the crux of the memories.

There was a long pause, then, "Foster raped you for nine weeks?" It was Quinn's voice, harsh, whispered.

I cut my eyes in his direction, then quickly looked back down at my hands. "Yes. Him and others. I don't know how many. It was mostly guards, mostly men, but not all." My voice was detached, as if I was relating a bad plot to a movie I wished I'd forgotten.

"What happened to him? To all of them?" he asked.

Shaking my head, I answered, knowing he wasn't going to like what I had to say. "Nothing. I didn't talk. It would have been my word against all of them. There was enough evidence to know something bad happened. Enough so that I could be moved someplace safer. But, like you said, Quinn. My parents were felons. Who would believe a thirteen-year-old con artist over another cop? Cops trust cops. That's always been *our* problem, hasn't it?"

I raised my eyes when I asked that question. I looked into Quinn's face and saw the narrowed eyes, the edges of white around his flared nostrils, the hard, straight line of his mouth. Oh he was angry, no doubt. I wasn't going to wait for him to say something...I wasn't finished. I poked my finger at his chest.

"You can't get over the fact that I was in jail, and I can't get over that you're a cop. I'm sick of your attitude. I was good enough to fuck, to put a notch in your holster, but not good enough for you to help me when I needed it."

I turned to Owen, breaking the connection with Quinn. "I'm tired Owen. I don't want to talk about this anymore. Not with Quinn here. It doesn't help. He just makes me feel dirty."

I heard the sharp intake of breath behind me, and wondered if I'd finally pissed Quinn off for good. Maybe he would leave me alone. He'd been treating me like a second-class citizen and I was tired of it. I'd worked hard since I was released from the CYA. It might not have been Quinn's idea of an upstanding job, but I'd been an entertainer, not a con artist.

The things they were doing in Juniper Springs were just a con on a different scale. So what if werewolves really existed? It didn't change the fact that the town was creating an illusion to bring in tourists in order to make money. The sheriff was just helping to perpetuate the lie.

"What do we need to do to break this spell or potion so I can go to bed?" I asked.

Owen looked over my shoulder at Quinn, and neither man spoke for a long minute. Finally, with a deep sigh, Quinn put his hand on my shoulder and I went stiff at the touch. "Look at me, Katie. Please," he added, softly.

I turned on the couch to face Quinn, but I scooted back and Owen repositioned himself so that I could press my back into his broad comfort. Owen snaked an arm around my waist, and I held on to it. I glared at Quinn. I was feeling vulnerable and a little bit scared. I spoke first.

"Let's get something straight, Quinn. According to what you've both told me, someone put a potion and a spell on me that would make me relive my darkest memories, in an effort to drive me insane. Is that right?"

Quinn nodded, and looked as though he wanted to add something.

I continued before he had a chance. "You said it was something personal, and I take that to mean someone close by. It had to be someone with access to my personal belongings. And it all started the night you threw me in jail. Quite a coincidence, considering the nature of my worst memories.

"It makes me wonder if you aren't the person who's doing this to me. Maybe that's why you're trying so hard to avoid touching me. It might let us see what you're doing. What I want to know is what you expect to get out of this? What do you hope to gain?"

"Don't, Katie," Quinn said quietly, his face pale. "I didn't do this to you. I wouldn't. God, I don't see you that way, at all. I should have told you why the curfew was important, that the werewolves were real. Christ, I was so scared when you called me from the Ranch on the night of the full moon. All I could think was to get out there and get you safe. If I could take back putting you in the cell I would. It was the only way I could be sure you wouldn't go back out there."

"G&O is the safe house, Quinn. You know that. Why didn't you bring her to us?" Owen asked.

Quinn glared at Owen, and if looks could kill, Owen would have dropped dead on the spot. He finally responded to Owen, even if he didn't answer the question. "Fuck you. You know why," he said. "And God help me, I was wrong!"

It was getting hard to breathe. With Owen pressed tight against my back, and Quinn leaning toward me, there was too much man in the room for me to think straight. I pushed to my feet, causing both men to lean back out of my way.

I wanted to run. Not run away, just go for a nice, long run, and have everything be back to normal when I returned. Neither Quinn nor Owen were acting as I expected them to act. Owen was all protective and had some sort of superior power, as if he was in charge of the situation. Quinn was acting jealous, even though we both knew he didn't feel that way about me. It was as though there was some long-standing competition between the two men. *Newsflash: I will not be a pawn in their game.*

Pushing aside their little pissing contest, I started to pace and to think. I hated the thought that someone wished me harm and had come close to succeeding. I really hated that I needed to somehow depend on these two men for protection against this magick. Despite what I said to Quinn, I didn't really think he was behind the attack. There was just something wrong with the emotions in the room. We were getting our signals and our words all tangled.

I turned to face the men and found them sitting next to each other, both turned toward me, both with hunger on their faces. I'd remarked once before how similar the two men were. Not similar as in brothers, but similar in build, similar in their movements, similar in the power that emanated from each of them. Right now, they were similar in their stillness.

I shivered, and not with the cold. I touched my fingertips to the spot on my neck where Quinn had left his mark. Owen had run his tongue over the marks when they were fresh. Shit. I knew there was much to discuss, but I needed this first question answered above all else.

"Are you a werewolf?" I asked, looking at Quinn. The question I really wanted answered was whether I was a werewolf after Quinn's bites, but it was easier to ask this way.

Quinn shook his head, and so did Owen beside him. It was really a bit eerie how much the two of them reminded me of each other. If I took the head shakes to mean neither of the men was wolfy, it still left the question of how they knew about spells and such.

"What are the two of you then? Wizards or something? Because I know you're something. I can feel the power that rolls from you. You know about spells. Can you perform spells, too?"

Again, both men shook their heads, and then Quinn buried his face in his hands. Not as though he were lying, but as though he just didn't want to talk any more. The atmosphere in the room was changing. It was electric, as if heat lightning was about to crackle over our heads.

Owen draped an arm over the larger man's shoulder, offering comfort when I hadn't realized any was needed. The two men sat together, hip touching hip, Owen's arm around Quinn. I stared, all anger suddenly turned into a white-hot desire.

I had a sudden flash of Quinn on his back, his beautiful hair spread over red satin sheets, his hard body stretched endlessly before me. Naked and most definitely interested. *What the fuck?*

Chapter Eighteen

This *was* a dream, wasn't it? I was standing in my living room, not naked in a bed with Quinn. I was still enough in control of myself to realize that this vision of Quinn was something other than real. Oh God, the dreams were coming for me again. I was breathing fast, first from the promise of pleasure, now from the beginnings of panic.

Quinn gently kissed me and chased away the edge of fear.

"Come back to me now, Katie," he whispered, his breath hot against my mouth.

Two pairs of arms held me upright. With one at my front and the other at my back, the realization that I was now part of a Quinn and Owen sandwich brought me all the way back to reality. I was still wearing Owen's shirt and Quinn was still in his blue jeans and tee. No one was naked and there were no red satin sheets.

Owen's long arms reached around me from behind, his hands resting lightly on Quinn's hips, keeping us all close. The warm cocoon of the embrace felt like the safest place in the world. Owen seemed content to hold me while Quinn chased away the dreams with gentle kisses.

The familiar earthy scent of Quinn mixed pleasantly with the equally elemental scent of Quinn. As if I were suddenly standing in the middle of a great forest, I inhaled sharply, drawing in the smells of pine, juniper, with an undertone of rich loamy soil. The kind I wanted to sink my hands into.

Quinn brushed his lips over mine once more then pulled back and stared at me, as though he was willing me to understand something. The message was lost to me in the sensations of the moment. I was drowning in pleasure, overwhelmed by the feel of these two men.

"Quinn? Owen? What's happening?"

Without answering, Quinn looked over my shoulder at Owen. I glanced up just in time to see their gazes meet in a flash of heat lightening that left the three of us scorched and the scent of ozone in the air.

Before I could pull back in shock, Quinn bent his head for one last kiss. Then he turned on his heel and left my apartment, closing the door firmly behind him.

****

Once Quinn left, Owen and I moved apart. I headed for the couch, he for the kitchen to pour fresh drinks. "Is the spell really broken? How do I know the memories won't come back the next time I sleep?"

"The spell is well and truly broken, KC. It couldn't stand against the powerful magick the three of us called.

The only dream likely to still linger is the one of your vision of Quinn."

I shivered, only half with pleasure. "What was that?" I whispered.

"Powerful magick," Owen answered just as softly, as he returned to sit near me on the couch. "You called magick, and his joined yours. Then I added mine." He shook his head before I could ask. "I can't tell you what you are, but there is an element of love to your magick. It's the same with Quinn and me. That's why the emotions were so raw, so confusing in here tonight."

I started to ask what magick, but Owen cut me off. "No, KC, I'll not tell you what kind of magick Quinn and I have. That's for after you discover your own."

I sighed. My naiveté was officially gone. Doubt and disbelief were luxuries I could no longer afford. Werewolves were real. Spells, potions, and witches were real. I was having real visions of the future when I told fortunes. What other fairy tales would turn out to be true? Vampires? Zombies? I tucked my feet up under me, sipped at my drink, and struggled to understand all that Owen was telling me.

Lightly brushing his fingertips over my arm, Owen continued. "There were two major elements to what happened to you. The potion made you susceptible to the spell. It lowered your natural psychic defenses. It wouldn't have taken much, just a few drops into your favorite lotion or in your soap. Something that your skin came into contact with everyday.

"It was the spell that truly was dangerous. The Dark Maker spell is a dark magick. Only a few people would have the ability and knowledge necessary to cast it. The spellcaster was powerful enough to keep the spell attached to you even after you left the area," Owen said.

"Who? Who would want to do this? Who *could* do it? The only witch I know is Amelia, and she brought me back here, so I don't think it's her," I said. "I don't know any other witches."

Owen looked at me strangely for a minute. "How do you know Amelia is a witch?" he asked.

"She isn't?" I gasped. "She said she was. Was she lying?"

Shaking his head, Owen allowed a small smile to tug at the corner of his mouth. "No, Amelia is definitely a most powerful witch. What I asked was, how do you know Amelia is a witch?"

"Because she told me," I said. I let the frustration in my voice show. I didn't like playing games and I didn't understand what it was that Owen wanted me to know.

"Exactly. She *told* you. Yet you are magickal enough that you should be able to sense when someone is a powerful witch. Close your eyes, KC. Think back over your encounters with Amelia, what can you sense—no, that's not quite right. What can you taste that is different about her? Have you met any others with that same…flavor?"

I closed my eyes and pictured Amelia in her glowing neon caftans. I tried to look past the fluff of her, to taste the essence. I poked around in the memories, tested the sense of her when we were in a room together. It was like staring at one of those hidden pictures. I could only see it one way. Then my inner gaze shifted and suddenly I could see another image of Amelia superimposed upon the first. It was a smoky and diffused light, a blurring of the edges. It didn't hide her, it was as though another layer had been added to the image of her in my mind.

I gasped and opened my eyes. "I can see it," I said excitedly. "It's like I'm seeing her through a different lens."

Owen smiled. "Yes. Now, think over others you've met since you've been here. Look for a pattern. Is there anyone else that has a similar layer?"

I started a hit parade of memories walking through my mind, picturing people I'd met since I'd been at the Honey House. The first hit came with a ghost.

"Joanne! I can see it with her, too."

Owen laughed delightedly, and I shivered at the sound of it. I pressed on. Not Gabrielle. Not Melissa.

"Oh my God—Susan!"

"Yes," Owen agreed. "Any others?"

"I've been through all the women," I said.

"A little biased, are we? How about the men?" Owen laughed.

Well, call me Miss Unenlightened. I hadn't even considered the men. I wasn't even going to think about Owen or Quinn. Comparing those two men to Amelia or Susan would be like comparing saber-tooth tigers and house cats. The women might be dangerous in their own rights, but their power was nothing to what I sensed from Owen or Quinn.

On to the others. Raymond, no. Jason, no. Malcolm…Merkham, no, no.

Another gasp. "Gregory!" I exclaimed.

"Very good. Now think of the three witches you know, examine their interactions with you, look at the layers, does one of them fit this act? Is one of the visions darker when it comes to you?"

Without thinking, I wanted to shout out Susan's name and Owen knew that. He slowed me with a finger against my lips and instructions to examine the memories first.

"Oh my God…" I said.

"Yes," Owen answered on an unhappy sigh. "Quinn is on his way there now."

Chapter Nineteen

Be careful what you ask for. I knew that better than most, but last night I hadn't been able to resist asking Owen about my recently gained sex appeal. I knew I was reasonably presentable, and I knew that my stand-offish vibes attracted a certain type of man. Those facts didn't help explain why every man who'd been in my apartment had made moves on me.

According to Owen, there was some sort of spell on the owner's apartment that interacted with my unique magick and affected the people who came into my personal space. He didn't seem particularly interested in learning more about the cause or about the effects. He said I could learn to live with it.

It wasn't exactly like a love potion, he'd explained, more like the lust that surrounded the goddess Aphrodite. I found that comparison extremely unsettling. He'd laughed at my discomfort and suggested I read Joanne's Book of Shadows to get a feel for the difference between spells, potions, and personal magick. Of course, he wouldn't tell me any more about my magick, just reiterated that I would discover it in time.

So this morning I was outside on the patio, eating my breakfast, and trying to read. Unfortunately, the focus necessary to read was absent. I was most definitely bothered by the things Owen had told me. Especially when I thought of my night with Quinn.

Had it taken some external influence to bring us together in such an intimate fashion? I'd been the one to crawl on his lap and initiate the activities. Somehow, given his obvious dislike of me, we'd spent a long night on the loving. To find out that maybe his passion was the result of a spell and he'd been unable to resist me? Gah! That left it feeling a lot like date rape.

Add to that the whole sexual goddess bullshit. It didn't matter where you put the emphasis. *Fucking* spell or fucking *spell*. None of the men were attracted because of *who* I was. It had more to do with *where* I was. It doesn't get any less flattering than that.

My coffee sloshed when I slammed the cup on the table, and I quickly moved the book out of the spill zone. I couldn't believe that on top of everything else, someone called the Dark Maker spell on me. Someone must really hate me.

I was determined to spend the day alone reading through the Book of Shadows until I found a way to remove whatever spell was within the walls of my apartment. I never wanted a command performance from a man again.

I was so lost in self-recriminations that I didn't even glance at the caller ID when my phone rang.

"KC," I snapped.

"KC, I'm sorry. I know my behavior was uncalled for. Can you forgive me?" asked an unfamiliar voice.

"Who is this?" I demanded.

"Edwin. Edwin Merkham. Don't hang up. I just want to apologize for my boorish behavior."

"Boorish behavior? Is that what you call kidnapping at gun point?" I snapped.

"I know. I was out of control. I let the story cloud my judgment. I'm sorry."

"All right, all right, you've apologized. Now what do you want?" I said, not worried about sounding polite.

"Yes...well. Uhm—"

"Spit it out."

"Right. It's like this, KC. The paper has asked me to tell your story in a more sympathetic light. I'd like to do it with your permission, but they're going to run the story, with or without you," he said, speaking fast.

"I already have the full details regarding your background and your foster parents. It's a classic tragedy of the failure of our system to protect defenseless children from predators like the Pattersons."

"Look, Merkham—" I broke off, thinking quickly. I needed to head this off as quickly as possible. I didn't want any more stories about me or Juniper Springs in the paper.

"It's Edwin, remember? I know you'd probably value your privacy more, but trust me, the paper is going to print this story. Look, this is harder over the phone. I need to head back north for a couple of days anyway. Are there any rooms available at the Honey House?"

It hadn't escaped my notice that it was time for the full moon again. Merkham had more than one reason he wanted to stay at the Honey House. I *wanted* to lie and tell him that there was no room at the inn. I *wanted* to suggest he'd be more comfortable at one of the chain hotels in Sedona. *I wanted to tell him to fuck off and die.*

"Yes," I answered on a resigned sigh. *Shit.*

****

Joanne's Book of Shadows was a hard cover journal, filled to overflowing with cramped handwritten notes. It was mostly organized as if it were a diary, with every entry in chronological order, starting shortly after she'd received the Honey House from Amelia. She'd recorded most of the spells in the back of the book, like a glossary. The content had been added from both the front and the back and eventually it had met in the middle. Notes spilled into the margins, until there was very little whitespace left. It might take me a lifetime to decipher all her notes.

Even though I was certain I wasn't a witch, it made sense to gather the information I was learning about spells and magick in one place so I'd taken Amelia's advice to start my own Book of Shadows. Instead of using my laptop, I decided to follow the traditional method of handwriting my notes. The limits of a bound journal were obvious, so I used a three-ring binder, instead. I added tabs for organizing and extra paper, in case I could think of anything I wanted to write. At this point, the only content in my book was the lunar table. I would never again lose track of the full moon. Not when so much was at stake.

I started thumbing through Joanne's book, opening to random pages, reading whatever captured my attention. Which was everything. Medicinal plants and herbs. Rituals and holidays. Witch's familiars. The difference between spells, wards, and intentions. There was so much to learn. And no shortcut to tell me what had been done to my apartment that was making me some kind of man magnet. I closed the book in frustration.

****

"We need your help, KC. We've been skirting the edge of discovery all year. As Liulfr for the pack, I have made some decisions that will be tough on our members. You can help ease the transition." Gabrielle was sitting next to him and holding his hand tightly.

The conversation lasted exactly twenty seconds before I was completely lost. Thirty minutes ago Raymond had shown up looking for Gabrielle. After a brief, whispered conversation, they'd pulled me into the library for a "talk."

"Raymond, I don't understand. Let's assume I don't have a clue what you're talking about—wait! Are you telling me *you're* a werewolf? And what's the pack Liulfr?" I asked, carefully pronouncing the word Lee-ulfer, as Raymond had said it. Minus the throaty growl, of course.

"I thought you knew I was a were. What did you think I was doing at the Ranch?" he asked.

"Okay, yeah, I suppose in abstract I realized you must be a...a..." I trailed off.

A snarl ripped through his chest, deep and menacing. It would have been terrifying without the grin splitting Raymond's expressive face and the sparkle in his eyes.

Who am I kidding? It *was* scary. My pulse raced as I tried to appear casual about the whole wolfy experience.

"Knock it off, Raymond. You're scaring her," Gabrielle said with a smack to the back of her husband's head.

Raymond ducked and laughed. "The Liulfr is the pack's shield, their leader or alpha, " Raymond answered rather dismissively. "I can explain pack law later, but right now, we need your help.

"Merkham called me a little while ago. He said that the newspaper has Jason's article about the Ranch and is printing it this weekend. He offered to let me comment for the record, to give me the chance to tell my side of the story. Without saying it directly, he'd implied the story definitely is a reveal of the werewolves.

"The pack needs you, KC," Raymond said. "Juniper Springs has been a safe place for us. We only started the Ranch because we were tired of always running, always moving on to another town when rumors started to spread. Here in Juniper Springs, we're just a different type of supernatural. There are so many other metaphysical happenings here that the wereanimals just blended right in with the others."

"Merkham is on his way here," I said. "He's going to be staying at the House."

"I know," Raymond said.

"She can't turn him away, the House won't like it," Gabrielle reminded Raymond.

"No, I know that. I just wondered if you would, you know, talk to him. Convince him not to report on this. At least not right now, give us some time."

"Raymond, if Merkham can prove werewolves exist, it will be the biggest news story ever! He isn't going to give up on it just because I ask nicely. Someone already killed Jason for the same thing.

"Tell me the truth. Did one of the werewolves kill Jason to keep the ranch a secret?" I asked.

"I'd wondered the same thing," Raymond said. "Believe me, I asked. Because I'd have dealt with it myself if one of my pack killed Jason. Don't get me wrong, I'd have hated it if Jason exposed us. Hell, that's what I'm trying to prevent now. No matter how big the stakes are, I wouldn't tolerate a cold-blooded murder."

It seemed a strange way to phrase it, but I let him continue.

"Jason came to see me the afternoon he returned," Raymond said, speaking fast, his voice a whisper. "He had a picture of Stevie, my youngest werewolf, just after he transformed. Stevie has trouble controlling the shift sometimes. I had taken him out to hunt and feed a few days before the full moon so his hunger would be sated. It lessens the blood lust in a new were. Jason got a lucky photo."

Gabrielle squeezed his hand, drawing his attention back to her. They stared at each other for a long moment and I could swear she shook her head slightly.

I said nothing, just waited for their silent communication to finish. I would have had a very hard time believing this whole conversation if Quinn and Owen hadn't confirmed that the werewolves were real. *Who am I kidding?* I was still struggling in the belief department. Acceptance isn't always the same as believing. I hadn't seen as of yet…and you know what they say about seeing is believing.

When Raymond turned back to face me, I said, "I still don't understand what you want me to do."

Gabrielle answered this time, "Try to find out what Merkham knows and what he's going to print. If he knows for sure about the werewolves, maybe you can give Raymond a head's up, let us get a head start," she said, squeezing Raymond's hand.

Raymond shook his head. "The world is getting much smaller these days. Merkham has pictures of us, Gabrielle. Now that he knows our identities, it would only be a matter of time before he tracked us down again.

"We all knew this day would come, that someday we'd have to make a stand. I'll notify—" he broke off abruptly. He cleared his throat, "I'll notify those who need to know, the other packs. No one else needs to be exposed. Then we can wait to see how it goes.

"We're still hoping you can convince him otherwise, KC, but we don't expect it. What we really need you to do is get him to delay his article for a week. That will give us enough time."

"There are other packs?" I asked, stuck on the first part of what he'd said.

Raymond laughed. "I don't know why it surprises me you ask, when we've always gone to such lengths to hide ourselves. Yes, there are at least two dozen packs across the US and hundreds more worldwide. This is not the first time weres have been threatened with exposure.

"In ancient times, it was easier to keep the werewolves a secret. If someone found out, you could try to either turn him or her through a bite or outright kill the threat. The old alphas carefully monitored how much attention their pack was drawing to their territory, and moved on if too many rumors started circulating. It's been our way for thousands of years, but we've all recognized that era is coming to an end. The Were Council—"

He smiled and broke off at my look of astonishment. "Yes, there is a governing Council that tries to keep the peace between the packs and protect the secret of our existence. So, the Were Council put into place a contingency for the first true exposure of werewolves. It looks like my pack will be the one to test it."

"What plan? What does that mean?" I asked.

"It would take about a month to get everyone out without it looking like a mass evacuation. Unfortunately, we don't have a month, so many will leave in the morning, after the full moon tonight. I arranged for my wolves to go somewhere…safe. We'll try to make the moves look as casual as possible, new jobs, elderly parents that need looking after, stories like that.

"A few of us will be the sacrificial lambs. We'll admit finally admit that werewolves do exist outside of horror movies. It will be our job to focus all the attention on our little pack and help give the impression that we are the last of the werewolves.

"Stevie will stay, because he's already been outed. And Gabrielle, of course."

"Wait! You're a werewolf, too?" I asked, my gaze shifting to the woman I'd worked beside for weeks.

Gabrielle laughed. "Of course I am! What did you expect? A monster?"

I shook my head. Nothing in this world was as it seemed. "Okay, how many others are staying?"

"For now, just the three of us, but I understand that a couple more werewolves want to join us. Some strong fighters who have their hungers well controlled. They should be here in a few days. We believe those of us who are outed will be in some danger from the constant attention we expect to encounter. We'll keep the pack limited to minimize the threat people may feel from acknowledging werewolves really do exist."

"Okay, pardon my ignorance, but how *dangerous* are you? I don't actually know what real werewolves do," I said.

"I do the beds and light cleaning, but prefer it when we bring in help for the windows," Gabrielle quipped.

"Smart ass," I said and threw a pillow at her head. Her hand was faster than I could follow when she snagged it out of the air, and I gasped.

"Seriously, KC, that's what we do. Whatever any other person does most of the time. We work, we play, we have normal lives. On the full moon, we transform. It's safer to stay away from normal humans when we've shifted, but mostly so we don't accidentally spread lycanthropy to someone. Most werewolves don't randomly eat people or attack without provocation.

"Very new werewolves sometimes find it hard to control their wolf form, so the more experienced pack members gather them up and teach them how to survive. The rest of us have a howling good time once a month and then go back to our regular lives," Gabrielle finished with a smile.

"It's not always so passive," Raymond added, his face more serious than Gabrielle's. "We can draw on our power and change whenever it's needed. A threatened werewolf can be forced to change involuntarily. The more powerful werewolves can change at will, or even only partially change. It all depends on the circumstances.

"Gabrielle and I have full control, as will any who join us later. Stevie is young, we'll have to be careful he doesn't feel too threatened in the crush of attention this admission draws to us. Once the initial excitement wears off, we'll quietly send Stevie to another pack, and get him away from the spotlight."

I didn't take time to think through my offer, I just knew it was the right thing, what the House wanted. "You need to move in here," I said. "Today. Now."

Raymond was shaking his head before the offer was out of my mouth.

"That won't work KC. It'll draw too much attention to you. Besides, we're going to have to bring Stevie to our house, until the new additions arrive. I know this will sound strange, but werewolves like to cuddle together when we're stressed, it gives us comfort. Having Stevie with us will make us all feel better."

"Raymond, you have to listen to me. Gabrielle, tell him. I know you can sense it, too," I said. A wave of desperation rolled through me.

Gabrielle looked at me, her dark eyes unreadable, face serious. Slowly, she turned to face her husband. "Raymond, what KC is trying to say is that it's not just her. The House wants us here now, too."

Raymond looked away from us for a minute, and then answered without turning back. "I know that we've learned over time not to question the House, but this makes no sense to me," Raymond said.

"Look, let's argue about it later. Merkham is on his way. Gabrielle, take suites one and two. The adjoining interior door will let you spread out, and should leave enough room for Stevie, too. Take suite three if you need it. That gives you the most privacy, since you'll be on the opposite side of the House from me.

"I'll put Merkham upstairs. He'll be gone in a day or two. Do whatever you want with the furniture, we have plenty of storage. Swap pieces, store stuff, whatever. We can worry about it later.

"Please, Raymond," I said, my voice near panic. "I can't explain this feeling; I just know something bad will happen if you're not here right now."

We all heard the car pull up in the drive. There were only a few seconds left before Merkham came inside for his room.

Gabrielle grabbed Raymond's hand and pulled him to his feet. "This is not the time or place to continue this discussion. Come, let me show you the rooms of which she speaks."

They were heading down the hall, away from the front door, when Merkham rushed in yelling, "Goddammit, KC! Why didn't you tell me there'd been another murder?"

A fist twisted around my heart. Someone else was dead. "Who?" I managed to croak out as I raced to the front counter.

"That jewelry store owner. Susan somebody...and they arrested that queer for her murder."

Chapter Twenty

I stood flatfooted, while Merkham rushed in the opposite direction, presumably toward his room, since I'd practically tossed a key in his direction. Pulling my cell phone from my pocket, I pushed the speed dial, thinking while I waited for an answer. *Susan dead? Gregory arrested?* I felt helpless, frustrated, and out of my element. *Why isn't Owen answering his phone?* I pushed the end button and blew out a breath.

I tried to feel something other than relief at Susan's death, but I just wasn't that damn charitable. Not that I'd actually wanted to kill her myself, but I would have liked a chance to kick her ass. With a snort, I gave that idea up. Physically, Susan had been a candy ass and there was no satisfaction in that. Magickally, Susan had been something else entirely.

From the moment we'd been introduced, Susan's holier-than-thou attitude had set my teeth on edge. Her possessive attitude toward Quinn gave me just the tool I'd needed to extract my own petty revenge. I winced when I realized I'd thought of Quinn as a tool in our initial skirmish.

It hadn't been Quinn who had sabotaged my evening with Jason, but the jealous bitch herself. I hadn't been a true threat at that point, so she'd just done a little interfering. I was sure she hadn't killed Jason. His murder had to be related to the werewolves. But the dead coyote on my back patio the same day I'd found Jason? Yeah, she'd have done that, mistakenly believing it would drive me away from the Honey House and Juniper Springs.

There was no way to anticipate that the discovery of the coyote would lead to a night of passion. Susan had been extremely pleased with herself when she'd seen me windblown and bedraggled on the back of the sheriff's bike. In fact, she'd even sold me the rose quartz, which was used to promote emotional healing. She'd probably been feeling sorry for me. Until she'd realized Quinn and I had slept together. That was the trigger for the Dark Maker spell. She must have been an extremely powerful witch with a very skewed sense of right and wrong.

I thought back to the first line of Joanne's Book of Shadows: *Harm no one.* Susan had violated that most basic principle of witchcraft. Was her death an example of the Rule of Magickal return? Seemed like karma to me.

I had a lot of questions and there was only one person who could give me the answers. With another deep sigh, I reluctantly pressed the speed dial for Quinn.

"KC, what's wrong? Are you all right?" Quinn barked.

My laughter sounded harsh, even to me. "No, everything's not all right. Is it true? Is Susan dead? Did you arrest Gregory?"

There was a long pause, and then Quinn asked, "Where are you?"

"I'm at the House. Merkham is back. He showed up here a few minutes ago and he told me about Gregory and Susan." I repeated my question from between clenched teeth. "Is it true?"

"KC, listen to me," Quinn said, his voice sounding strained. "I'll come over tonight and explain everything, but it won't be until much later. I need you to stay inside, honor the curfew.

"Keep Merkham at the House. Tell him I'll arrest him if he goes near the Ranch or anywhere else tonight. Hell, tell him I'll shoot him! Just whatever you do, please stay inside. I've got to go, KC. I'll be there later. Gregory is fine. He'll be fine." The connection ended.

I stared at the suddenly dead phone. Would I ever understand Quinn? He sounded concerned about me, almost panicked at the thought of my going out to the Ranch under the full moon tonight. The man left me reeling, not something I enjoyed. I wanted my men uncomplicated, a word that seemed to be the antithesis of Quinn. It hadn't escaped my notice that he still hadn't answered any questions, just made a vague promise of coming by sometime later. That thought brought an unwelcome shiver that started low in my belly and spread to my most intimate parts. *Shit.*

The front door slammed, pulling me from thoughts of Quinn that I didn't want to have. I ran to the front of the house already aware I'd never reach him in time. I raced through the hallways and spilled onto the porch. I was just in time to watch helplessly as Merkham's car turned onto the main road. Then my heart sank. There was another vehicle in the distance. The big, black truck that belonged to the big, bad wolf leader. Merkham was following Raymond. *Was Gabrielle in the truck, too?* Of course she would be. Tonight was the full moon. They were probably on their way to have a howling good time together.

Gabrielle had made it sound as though there was no danger, but I didn't think that was exactly true. From what I'd learned earlier, they all shifted at the full moon, but the biggest danger wasn't necessarily that they'd eat someone, but more that the lycanthropy might spread. Raymond said he and Gabrielle had full control. Didn't that imply there were others who didn't have control? No one had ever answered when I'd asked how many werewolves there were in Juniper Springs. I only knew of three: Raymond, Gabrielle, and Stevie.

Stevie didn't have control. G&O was a safe house, there was a curfew for the whole town. There had to be some danger if such precautions were necessary.

All these thoughts ran through my mind even as I raced to change my clothes. Jeans, hiking boots, and a long sleeved sweatshirt were the best I could do to protect against the brush and random werewolf scratches.

If someone wanted to eat me…well, that's what the gun was for. At least my trip to the Los Angeles area hadn't been a total waste of time. I went to my nightstand and removed the nine mil hidden in the false front of a book. *War and Peace, what else?*

Call me superstitious, but I didn't think it was a good idea to go to a werewolf ranch without silver bullets.

****

I thought over my options and decided it made little sense to track Merkham through the woods. He would probably park along the outskirts and hike to the trailer, just like last time. He was here for the werewolves and he wouldn't stop until he had proof they existed. This was his big journalistic break and he would want pictures.

Assuming I knew his goal, I decided to make up for his head start by driving into the compound to park on the far side of the trailer. Maybe I could hide in the trees to wait for Merkham to hike in. Hopefully, no stray werewolf would eat either of us before moonrise. That would be bad publicity, all the way around.

I followed the dirt road to the trailer and found Merkham's car parked next to Raymond's truck. So much for my plans. Merkham was already here and I was late to the party.

I flipped my phone out to call and warn Quinn about Merkham, only to realize he probably hadn't ended his call as abruptly as I'd thought earlier. The battery was dead. *Shit.* I tossed the useless phone into my truck and shut the door. This was completely stupid, but I couldn't leave Raymond and Gabrielle to fend for themselves.

There was a faint glow to the west, but the night sky was deepening, and it would soon be full dark. Until the bright full moon took over the night. I had to get Merkham away from here before moonrise.

I stepped away from the truck, listening hard, trying to catch any hint of sound from the others. The only sound was the rustle of branches as the wind caressed the trees. I moved forward cautiously, pausing every few steps to listen again. How could it be so still? They couldn't have beaten me here by more than ten or fifteen minutes. The trailer was locked and silent; nothing indicated they'd gone inside. *Where was everybody?*

"Hello? Edwin Merkham, are you out here? Can you hear me?" No response. Even the wind seemed to pause for a moment so that the only sound I heard was the blood pulsing in my ears.

Coming to a decision and getting my bearings in the fading light, I walked quickly into the woods. I would walk a tight perimeter just inside the tree line. I was a city girl, I didn't know anything about tracking people in the woods, but maybe I could find a clue as to which way they'd gone. The dried brush crunched beneath my boots as I passed between the trees, staying hidden in the deepening shadows of twilight.

I caught a flicker of movement from somewhere in front of me. *What was that?* Another flash, a bit of light between the shadows. Could that be Merkham's white shirt as he moved through the trees? I quickened my pace.

Snap. Crackle. Pop. Those sounds didn't used to be so scary, but they were now. A dried branch cracked close by. I whipped my head around but didn't see anything, but I knew—there was something behind me. *Shit! Some big, brave rescuer I'm turning out to be!*

I sped up. I didn't want to lose whoever was in front of me and didn't want to be caught by whatever was behind me. When the figure spilled out into the parking area, I followed, without hesitation. *What the hell?*

Raymond stood in front of me, looking just as surprised as I must have looked.

Raymond must have realized his mistake as quickly as I had, because we both whirled around to look at the woods just as Merkham stepped into the clearing. He held a gun pointed right at the two of us.

Fuck! Merkham had replaced his little twenty-two with a nine mil. I knew, because it matched the one hidden in the waistband of my jeans. Merkham's smile was as satisfied as any cat, having finally cornered his mouse.

All I could think to do was bluff, bluff, bluff.

"Oh, thank God, Edwin! There you are! Come on, we've got to go before Quinn gets here. He said he'd shoot us if we came back out here on the full moon." I took a step toward him and he fired at my feet. Dirt and dust kicked up everywhere. My heart thudded in my chest. *Shit!*

"Both of you stay right there until I tell you to move," Merkham said.

"Let her go," Raymond said. His voice was deeper with more growl than I'd ever heard before.

"Ah, yes. Well, that *will* be a problem. I have plans, and they include the *most* unfortunate Miss Carmichael," Merkham said.

I didn't like the sound of that at all.

Chapter Twenty-one

"If you'll both be so kind as to walk to the trailer. Stay close together now. KC, you in front. Raymond, you follow behind her. I want you both on the ground in front of the stairs," Merkham said. He used his gun hand to point. Sloppy. Maybe I would get a second chance to kick his ass.

He kept a safe distance behind us and ordered us to stop when we got about fifteen feet from the trailer stairs. "Sit down, right there. Put your hands in your laps," he said. His voice sounded excited, and he wore a grin on his face. It occurred to me he probably wasn't quite sane.

"Quinn will be here soon, Edwin. Why don't you and I get in your car and head back to the House?" I asked, keeping my voice reasonable. I was still trying to pass this off as a misunderstanding.

Merkham's grin widened. "Quinn won't be here. He has a murder to solve, and thanks to me, he has a very good suspect. He'll be busy tonight."

Something about that statement made my blood run cold. "Edwin? Do you know something about these murders?" I asked.

"Who knows what's going on in Juniper Springs? There are all kinds of mysterious happenings," Merkham said, a grin splitting his face.

"I know nothing preternatural killed Jason," Raymond said.

"True," Merkham said, "but there's enough circumstantial evidence that I can link it to the werewolves that I'm about to expose. The second murder will make it even more convincing that there's a cover up happening in Juniper Springs. The sheriff can't do much about it. Not unless he wants to look like he's involved in the conspiracy.

"What conspiracy?" I asked.

"Why, whatever it is that's been causing this town to shut down every full moon, of course," Merkham said. He looked up and over the treetops for a second before his gaze returned to us. I realized he'd done that at least twice now. From the direction and angle of his glance, I assumed he was looking for the moon. Each time he looked away from us, his gun hand wavered.

I sighed. "There's no way to convince you the werewolves aren't real, is there?" I asked.

"None," he grinned. "I *did* see Jason's pictures, you know. The first photo showed old Raymond here with a young man. The next three showed a shocking transformation. Suddenly, the young man was gone, and a giant wolf was in his place. The photos and article were very well done, actually. Too bad for Jason. His editor felt the need to kill the story," he giggled. "Not to worry though, the story *will* be told, only much more dramatically."

I felt Raymond move beside me, but Merkham saw it, and flicked the gun in his direction. "Don't move,

Martinez. We all know what you are. I would be completely justified in killing you here and now. It's clear that I'm terrified. Of course, I'd probably accidentally shoot KC, too. So really, I think staying still is your best option. Don't you?"

I didn't think he looked very terrified of getting eaten by the werewolf. In fact, he looked excited. He was seeing the Pulitzer Prize dancing right in front of him, and we were his party tickets. Then his words penetrated my brain and I felt sick.

"You *saw* Jason's photos?" I asked, suddenly flooded with knowledge.

Merkham nodded, his eyes sparkling.

"When was the last time you saw Susan?" I asked slowly.

"Clever girl. I want at least one person to know how creative I've been, and I suppose it doesn't matter much if I tell you, since you won't live beyond moonrise. The last time I saw Susan was when I killed her. She saw me here with Jason when I was supposed to be in Phoenix.

"The arrogant bitch thought she could blackmail me!" Merkham said, sounding affronted.

Actually, I couldn't argue with the arrogant or the bitch part, Susan was certainly both. Still, the death penalty for those two failings seemed a bit harsh. Since Merkham was in a mood to talk, I didn't interrupt to tell him what I thought.

Merkham continued. "I wanted Jason to look like a wolf kill, but I don't think I was very successful. Since I didn't know what an actual werewolf kill looked like, I just cut away the wounds. I was hoping people would assume the killer was a werewolf and he'd cut away any evidence of claw or fang marks." He looked pensive for a moment, as if judging how he could have done better.

Saliva pooled in my mouth and I fought not to throw up. He was so matter-of-fact about the killings, about cutting into Jason's body.

"Killing Susan was easier; I really didn't like her. Did you know just how much she hated you, KC? Why didn't you tell me about the little break-in and the dead coyote? She meant for you to die with her little spell. She tried to cast the same spell on me, but it didn't take. Turns out you have to have a conscience for that one to work. Nasty spell, I hear. Really, KC, I did you a favor getting rid of her.

"There is no danger of tying Susan's murder to me. It was such a simple thing. I just waited until Gregory and his fairy boyfriend were busy with customers. Then I snuck into their kitchen and took a knife from the dishwasher. Since Gregory does all the catering and cooking, I figured it was a sure bet his fingerprints would be on the knife. Believe me, I was very thorough.

"I'm getting better, don't you think? This time the wolf really will kill you, then I can kill him and I'll have my proof," he finished, his face glowing with pride at his cleverness.

I swallowed. "What do you mean?" I asked. My voice came out strong. Score one for the good guys.

"Oh, KC," Merkham said, sounding disappointed in his star pupil. "I thought you had this all figured out.

We're going to sit here and wait for the moon to rise. When Raymond transforms, he's going to eat you, and then I'll kill him. Oh, and I'll take pictures of course, while I wait for the mighty Quinn to arrive. But the sheriff will be too late to save either of you."

That he'd thought this all out was too disturbing for words. The man was a stone cold sociopath.

He gave a self-satisfied sigh. "I am a made-man, my Pulitzer awaits. Then an exclusive book deal. Maybe I'll buy the Honey House from your estate, KC. I can live in luxury in the place that made me famous. I'll drink to you every day," he said and made an imaginary toast.

Merkham looked up for the moon again and I got an idea. It was time to see just how psychic I was. I would try to talk with Raymond, mind-to-mind.

"Raymond, can you hear me?" I yelled in my mind. I was feeling rather foolish about the experiment. At least I was feeling foolish until Raymond's head jerked back.

"Fuck, KC. Don't shout. I didn't know you could talk this way. You're not a shapeshifter," he answered, his voice softer than a whisper inside my head.

"Sorry," I thought. *"Is this better?"* I mentally whispered. Okay, this rated right up there with Most-Bizarre-Things-I've-Ever-Done.

"Yes," he answered. *"I won't hurt you. Are you afraid?"*

"A little." I answered honestly. *"But since I've never seen a real werewolf, I'm not really sure what to expect. Is there any way you can reach Merkham before he could shoot you? Are you that fast?"*

"No, not before he could shoot me," Raymond answered.

"Then we have to disrupt his plan, force him to go out of order. Are you really good enough to transform whenever you want?" I asked, remembering his assurance that his ability to transform was under control.

His smile whispered through my head. *"I'm really that good,"* he said.

"Then let's put on a show. I'm going to kick your ass, and you're going to back me toward Merkham. You go ahead and transform whenever you think the time is right, but we need to move quickly. He'll hesitate to shoot us before you shift because that would deviate from his plan. He needs this to be a werewolf kill, so we'll have an advantage for a little while. Whichever of us can get closest to him needs to take him out. Go for his gun hand, he's sloppy. If you knock his gun away before I do, then get out of range because I've got a gun, too," I thought.

Raymond's gaze shot over to me then, his glance seemed to be an involuntary reaction to my last thought. Then the wind shifted and his nostrils twitched. *"Fuck! Go KC, go now!"* he urged, his words suddenly a roar in my head.

"What the fuck are you two up to?" Merkham yelled, and he glanced back up, probably looking for the moon again.

The horizon was brightening, moonrise wouldn't be long now.

I stood quickly. "I'm not going to just sit here and wait for you to kill me," I said to Raymond. He stood and started to circle me, as if sizing me up.

A feral growl spilled from Raymond's still human-looking lips. His thoughts pushed out passed me, toward the tree line, *"Goddammit, Gabrielle, get him out of here!"*

The skin on the back of my neck tightened, and a shiver passed over me. Gabrielle was out there with someone else. Someone Raymond didn't want around. We needed to move faster.

I feigned left, and Raymond was just there suddenly. I moved back with a squeal, and only part of me was acting. The other part began to be very afraid. Raymond growled again, and his skin began to ripple over his muscles. He took another step toward me, and I stepped back.

Then everything happened at once. I heard noises in the trees, branches and twigs snapping, warning growls, whining. Merkham started yelling at us to get back or he'd shoot. Another voice yelled, "Drop it!"

There was a sudden blast of heat and standing in front of me was the biggest wolf I'd ever seen. *Raymond.*

I pushed aside all of my concerns and focused on Merkham. His attention was divided between the commotion in the woods, the voice coming from behind him, and Raymond's wolf form. He never even realized the real threat was the woman he'd so casually planned to kill. Me.

With a sharp scream, I leaped into the air and let my legs fly out in a controlled kick. I hit Merkham on the right side of his head just as gunshots exploded all around us.

Chapter Twenty-two

When the dust settled, there were three bodies on the ground and a giant russet-colored wolf blocking my way to them. His hackles rose and a low, deadly growl rumbled deep in his chest. This had to be Stevie, and there was no sign he was in control. In fact, judging from his quivering muscles and snarling maw, he was getting ready for a midnight snack. *Me.*

A massive black wolf lay on the ground in a pool of blood. His eyes were closed, mouth open, and he was panting shallowly. Gabrielle knelt beside him, and spoke rapidly in Spanish. I only caught some of the words, but I thought she told him to wait to change.

Merkham lay near them, his upper chest a bloody mess. Everything had switched to slow motion when Merkham pointed the gun at Raymond. I was spinning, he was firing, then my gun was in my hand, safety off, and I'd fired as he'd already been stumbling sideways from my kick. He'd hurt more than one of mine and I hadn't hesitated to take him out. I'd placed three shots in a line down the center of his chest, as if each shot caught him as he was falling backwards. He wasn't going to hurt anyone ever again.

I hadn't looked at the third body yet. I couldn't. Not now. I knew who it was, and any help was a long ways off, if I couldn't get the situation with the werewolf under control.

The wolf moved slowly toward me, blue eyes grown dark with hunger, maw gaping, growl constant. Another quick glance at Gabrielle and Raymond confirmed I was on my own. I shivered. There were already enough bodies on the ground. Goddamn Merkham for putting us all in this situation. It wasn't Stevie's fault he'd been turned or that Jason had discovered the wolves. He shouldn't have to pay with his life. I kept my gun at my side.

"Stevie…you're Stevie, right? You don't need to do this. You *can* control your wolf," I said.

I was relieved to note that my voice sounded confident. I was about to run the most important con of my life. If I wanted to sell it to Stevie, then I needed to sound as if I believed it, too.

Raymond and Gabrielle were coming home with me— that made them mine. Following that logic, since Raymond was the pack's alpha, meant that in a twisted way, all of the werewolves were mine.

My heart filled again with the certain knowledge that I was supposed to protect what was mine. I would not kill Stevie. Power welled up within me with that thought. I gasped at the sensation of heat that spread through me. It was as though my blood now pumped ten degrees warmer. I was here as protector.

Stevie lunged, shattering my newly inflated sense of well-being as I scrambled to get out of his way. He leaped again and this time he caught a scrap of my sleeve as his paw brushed against my arm. He landed on all fours and turned to face me. The wolf snarled, jaws snapping, and he came at me a third time.

I turned, twisted, and moved out of his path with ease. With a jolt, I realized the wolf was too slow for me. Too slow? *How is that possible?*

A low growl raised the hair on the back of my neck as he started toward me again, belly slung low to the ground. He was stalking me.

Without thinking, I used the inner voice, the one I'd used just minutes ago to converse mind-to-mind with Raymond.

"Stevie! No more. You will not attack," I shouted with my mind. *"Back down. Now!"*

With a whimper, Stevie dropped his head and cocked an ear to one side. He looked unsure as to how he was hearing my voice in his head. Who could blame him?

With his haunches quivering, he lowered his muzzle to the dirt. His eyes shifted down and away, glancing back up at me every few seconds. It was a posture of complete submission.

We needed help. I needed to get to someone's cell phone and fast, but I couldn't if I had to watch Stevie the whole time. I had to be sure he wouldn't attack if I shifted my attention away from him.

I didn't yell, just spoke quietly in his head. *"Stevie, it's going to be okay,"* I thought. *"Go to Raymond, to your alpha. Help Gabrielle. You're going to be fine, no one will hurt you."*

Stevie rose with another whimper and slunk his way over to where Gabrielle was cradling Raymond in her lap. Stevie nuzzled at Raymond, his attention now completely focused on his injured pack leader. Gabrielle pulled Stevie's head down closer to Raymond and I could finally run to where my heart wanted me to go all along. To where that third body lay too still on the ground. *To Quinn.*

Blood soaked Quinn's chest, but I searched his pockets first, desperate to find his cell phone. Basic first aid: call for help. There wasn't anything I could do for a chest wound, we needed an ambulance. Then a movement caught my eye and I looked across to Gabrielle surrounded by two giant wolves. *Shit.* The wolves would be in danger if I called the 9-1-1.

I found the phone and saw the missed call displayed on the small screen. Owen. The phone rang before I could dial for help.

I pressed the answer key, and Owen's voice came in a rush. "Tell me where you are, KC," he demanded.

"The Way They Were," I answered. "Please hurry." I resisted the urge to ask how he knew I was the one answering, since I was using Quinn's phone.

"Is anyone armed?" Owen asked.

"Just me, now. Everyone else is down," I answered. "Owen, hurry. Raymond and Quinn have both been shot. There's a werewolf here, too. Or three of them, I guess.

Gabrielle is in her human form, and Raymond and Stevie are wolves," I said.

I closed my eyes, willing Owen not to ask any more questions.

"Keep your gun down," Owen said and he stepped through the trees, not more than fifteen feet away from me.

I dropped the phone in relief and started removing Quinn's shirt, looking for the source of all that blood. Owen hurried across the lot, but Stevie pushed to his feet, clearly intending to protect the pack alpha. Stevie's low growl carried clearly in the night air.

Speaking with my mind once more, I said, *"Stevie, we need him. I need you to let him pass."* With another shake of his big head, the russet wolf circled back around to crouch next to Gabrielle and Raymond.

As soon as Stevie turned away, my attention shifted to the unconscious Quinn. His face was deathly pale, as the life force within him soaked onto the hard packed soil. Fear gave me a desperate strength and I ripped Quinn's shirt from his body. I used the ruined cloth to wipe at all the blood, I needed to get a look at the wound.

"Come on, Quinn, stay with me. Come on, baby. I'm not going to let you go, now. You're going to be okay. Hold on."

I continued to murmur nonsense phrases as I explored the extent of his injuries. It looked as though there was one large hole, just above his left nipple. I needed to turn him, to see if the bullet had gone all the way through. I didn't know if I was trying to staunch the blood from one wound or two. From the mount of blood, I knew we couldn't have much time. We needed to get him to the hospital, now.

"Where's your car, Owen? Or better yet, let's take the patrol car. We don't have time to wait for an ambulance."

Owen looked at me for a long moment and I wanted to scream at him to hurry. I was not going to let him tell me that it was too late. I would not lose Quinn!

With a slight smile, Owen knelt beside me and passed a hand over Quinn's chest. "You'll heal now, Quinn," he said and then he whispered some other words in a language I didn't recognize.

Quinn's eyes fluttered open, blinking rapidly as if he was trying to see something that wasn't there. Owen pressed a hand to Quinn's forehead, and said, "Heal, my friend. I must tend to the others, now."

Owen stood, and said, "Gabrielle, I need to get to Raymond. Stevie, please. You must let me by."

"Yes," I added silently, and then I turned my attention from the wolves to focus on the honey gold eyes that were looking up at me.

"Quinn, I need to call an ambulance. I need to call the cops, too. Merkham's dead."

"Shhh, Katie. Just kiss me," he whispered, and his hand reached for the front of my shirt to pull me down.

I pressed my lips softly against Quinn's, a gentle touch to let him know I was glad he was alive. Quinn tangled his hand in my hair and pulled me against his lips in a hot, soul-claiming kiss that had nothing to do with gentle. His kiss was an affirmation of life. Quinn was alive. We would survive this night to fight another. He pushed his tongue into my mouth, drawing me in. It was as though he was feeding from me and I felt an energy flow between us. My newfound power was filling him, healing him.

One minute, Quinn was a bloody mess on the ground, the next he was savaging my mouth. I pulled back, breathless from the kiss, worried I might be hurting him. Quinn quirked his mouth, a smile tugging at his lips.

"Stopping now is probably a good idea," he said a bit breathlessly. "I need to call this in, take care of business before we go any further."

"What are you talking about?" I asked. "You need to be in the hospital. That wasn't a bug bite, you've been shot!"

Quinn pushed to his knees, then stood up, pulling me with him, "Have I really?" he asked.

Owen joined us then, and ran his fingers over Quinn's bloody but unblemished chest. "Nicely healed, friend," he said.

"Yes," Quinn said, and to my complete shock, he planted a quick kiss on Owen's mouth, and another on mine. "I owe both of you. Now, get out of here so I can do my job. There are things I must take care of, people I need to call."

"Quinn," I started to protest. He cut me off.

"Katie, I need your gun and your truck keys. Owen, I need your shirt. Take Katie home, and then go get Gregory," he added and handed Owen a key. He turned back to me, and said, "I'll stop by as soon as I can."

Before I could protest further, a now naked-from-the-waist-up Owen wrapped me in his arms and the world as I knew it blinked away.

Chapter Twenty-three

Nonplussed. Bewildered. Flummoxed. How in the hell could I even begin to describe how I was feeling? I was sure that only a moment ago I'd been standing in the dirt lot that surrounded the office of The Way They Were, talking with Quinn and Owen. Now, I stood looking around my living room, trying to make sense of the world.

"Owen?" I began, my voice sounding shaky to my own ears. "How did we get here? What the fuck just happened?"

Owen gave me a sexy wink, and in an exaggerated Irish brogue said, "Aye, don' be tellin' me ye've ne'er heard of the wee folk and our nefarious ability to whisk young maidens away to do our bidding."

"Not funny, Owen. How did we get here? Or, wait. *Are* we here? Is this some kind of mind game?" I asked. My mind didn't find anything funny or game-like about the situation, but I knew my brain would struggle to try to make reason out of the existing insanity it was facing.

"KC, look around. Touch anything you like. This is your place. I wouldn't have chosen to let you find out about me like this, except Quinn was right. This was an emergency and we needed to get you away from there.

"Raymond, Gabrielle, and Stevie will also be long gone before anyone else arrives. Quinn will make it look as though Merkham was trespassing and drew a weapon when confronted. It's going to be a lot easier to explain a justified police shooting than it would be to explain that an armed civilian killed him. Even if the victim was an obnoxious member of the press."

Owen stared off into the distance for a minute before continuing. "I'm afraid the story of the werewolves will still need to come out. We'll need to expose the wolves to explain why Merkham killed Jason and Susan. Otherwise, Quinn would be vulnerable to charges of conspiracy and murder."

I shook my head, trying to clear away Owen's comments about the wolves. What I really needed to know right this minute was how I'd arrived at my house.

"Owen!" I shouted.

Owen's head shot up and he just looked at me for a long moment before he crossed the floor to take me in his arms. Cradled against his chest, I could hear the steady beat of his heart.

"I'm sorry, KC. I was teasing you and then I got distracted. You deserve an answer." He led us to the couch, and took my hands in his.

"I did answer your question, you know," he said with a half smile.

"What? The wee folk bit? Right." I snorted.

"Well not all of us are so very wee. You've already accepted that there are things in this world such as werewolves and witches. Is it such a stretch to imagine that the Fae are real, too?"

"Okay, wait. *You're a fairy?*" I sputtered. I'd been through too much tonight to take any more of his teasing. I'd killed a man. I'd spoken to a wolf. Then my thoughts slowed as I put another piece of the puzzle together.

I'd watched Owen heal a man who should have died.

My gaze flashed upwards to meet his steady gray eyes. "You healed Quinn with some words and your hand."

"Yes," he said.

"And then you what? Just thought us here and so we were?" I asked, my voice rising with every impossible word.

"More or less," he said.

"More or less? What the hell does that mean?" I was trying not to shout, but failing dismally.

"Look, KC, it's just how we can move, that's all. It's like shifting a dimension. Not as complicated as a thought. I'm just one place and then I picture where I want to be next and I am. I don't use it a whole lot because I've chosen to live here as a human. Sometimes, like tonight, it comes in handy. It's how I was able to get to you, to get to Quinn so quickly." He shrugged, and looked away for a minute.

When he turned back, his face was impassive, but his voice was gentle. "I need to go get Gregory. Do you want me to come back tonight to answer your questions? Or maybe a little time to process everything would be better?"

"Is Gregory—" I started, but Owen cut me off with a shake of his head.

"No, he's a powerful witch. That's enough for him. He knows what I am and he loves me anyway. I wonder…will love ever be enough for you, KC?" Owen softly asked.

"What is that supposed to mean?" I asked, my anger spiking.

Owen stood and pulled me to my feet, before wrapping me in his arms once more. "Nothing. I just don't want to see you push people away who would love you. I'm sorry, KC. I need to go get Gregory and you need rest after you get cleaned up. This will wait. Gregory and I will be here tomorrow. And KC?"

"Yes," I answered automatically, my mind already shutting down against the impossibilities Owen was asking me to believe.

"Take the time to think about everything that's happened. Everything that you've learned, everything that you've done and seen. It is important. Good night, sweetheart." He kissed me lightly on top of the head, released me, and then with the lightest of pops, disappeared from the room.

****

Thinking about all that happened leant a nightmarish quality to the memories. Unfortunately, I knew it wasn't a dream. As soon as Owen had popped out, or whatever it was fairies did, I'd thrown away my torn and bloody clothes, scrubbed until I was raw, and then waited. Waited to feel something for killing a man. Waited to feel shock that fairies existed. Waited for Quinn to come.

Nothing happened. After a while, I'd tried to sleep, but that didn't happen either. So, I'd read Joanna's diary, used my laptop to research the Fae, and finally sat on the back patio looking out at the moonlit landscape until dawn blushed the sky.

Now, I followed my usual routine, putting out fruit and yogurt, bagels and coffee, and generally bustled around the kitchen and dining room, feeling lost. I never heard the door open, but suddenly I knew he was there. I turned and saw Quinn, framed in the light, his sun-kissed hair loose around his shoulders.

"Katie," he said, as he moved toward me.

Without any other words, Quinn swept me into his arms and carried me all the way through the House to my bedroom. Once there he held me up against his body, chest-to-chest. His arms wrapped around me, my arms were around his neck, and my feet dangled. Our gazes met, and I knew he was seeing the relief I felt at having him whole and unharmed. I felt the unfamiliar sting of tears and I looked away so he wouldn't notice.

Damn the man, he noticed anyway. He slid me slowly down the front of his body so that his glorious erection rubbed against my belly as he lowered me to the floor. As soon as my feet were steady, Quinn dropped to his knees and pressed his head to my chest. With his strong arms around me and his silky hair caressing my skin, the enormity of what I'd nearly lost overwhelmed me and I began to cry in earnest.

I couldn't explain the rush of emotions. Relationships were impossible without both trust and love. My ability to love died when I was three, along with my real family, so I knew I didn't love Quinn. My ability to trust had died with the rapes when I was only thirteen, and I would never again trust anyone completely.

Maybe that's what Owen had meant by his cryptic remarks. Even if I allowed myself to feel something for Quinn, I would never lower those shields enough. Maybe my tears were for myself.

"Shh, Katie, everything's all right. We're both safe," he stroked my hair and looked up at me with eyes that were liquid pools of gold. "We can talk later. I need to make love to you," he said.

I nodded, my throat too tight to speak.

Quinn helped me to fall gently back onto the bed, and kept himself between my legs. He pulled his own clothes off first, so that I could see the perfection of his chest. The soft brown curls brushed like silk over golden velvet skin. There were no wounds, no scars where the bullet had bit into him the night before. Owen's Fae powers were remarkable.

I sat up, lifted my shirt over my head, and then slid out of my shorts, taking my underwear with them. Quinn's kiss was as gentle as a butterfly as he lightly brushed his lips against mine. His fingers traced over my mouth, across my jaw line, and over the contours of my cheeks.

He cupped my face in his big hands, and I closed my eyes at the sensation.

The questions that plagued me through the night were washed away in a wave of desire. I was drowning in Quinn. My body felt alive, energized, and hungry. God, yes, that was the word…hungry. I was starved for a taste of the man.

Quinn pulled back slightly so he could look at me, which gave me the chance to study him in return. He was so beautiful, his strong face looked regal in the early morning light. The amber eyes were dark with passion, sculpted lips were parted, his full lower lip caught by his teeth. Oh yes, I wanted him and without a doubt, he wanted me, too.

His thumbs brushed at the remnants of my tears, then he kissed the tip of my nose, each eyelid, my forehead. The rough calluses of his hands were so at odds with the gentleness of his touch.

"Katie," he said again, his voice a hoarse whisper. Then his mouth began to move. Down my neck, across my collarbone, lower to my breasts. He left a blazing trail of kisses, gentle bites, and velvety licks. His hands moved to cup my breasts, and when his mouth clamped on one nipple, his fingers rolled and pinched the other.

The breath slammed against my lungs, struggling to escape the self-imposed restraint I hadn't even realized I was holding on to. I'd been treating Quinn as though he was still hurt, as though his near-death experience had weakened him. It hadn't and I needed him now.

A desperate desire bloomed inside me. There was no room for gentle touches or loving caresses. I wanted to feel…to *know* he was alive. I tangled my fingers into his hair and pulled him harder against my breasts. He caught my new sense of urgency and met my desperation with tongue and teeth.

"Yes," I moaned, and arched into his touch when he drew my nipple hard into his hot mouth. He pushed my breasts together, his mouth alternating working both nipples, tongue following the cleavage his hands created.

"Oh God," I whispered. "I need you inside me, right now," I gasped.

Quinn slid down my body, wrapped his arms around my legs, and draped my calves over his forearms. He muttered, "Not yet. I have to taste you first. You can't deny a starving man." Then his tongue slid into my pussy.

My breath escaped in tiny, whimpering gasps as Quinn fucked me with his tongue, slick and hot, in and out. My hips moved against his mouth, and still I needed more. I shuddered, full of desire. Quinn licked me from top to bottom, long, seductive strokes. The tension from the night was melting away under his clever tongue.

"More," I begged greedily.

With a small laugh, Quinn's tongue went to work while his fingers glided, pumping, demanding. He brought me to the edge of orgasm, spilling me over, and quickly withdrawing. I wanted to whimper at his abrupt departure, until he flipped me over onto my stomach.

There was no more teasing now. Quinn was as desperate as I was. He guided the broad tip of his cock against my pussy, and then pressed himself inside.

A moan of pure pleasure slipped out at the overwhelming sense of completeness I experienced with Quinn filling me.

"You're mine, Katie. I carry part of you inside me now, you will never be able to forget me," his voice a low growl in my ear.

It was a completely barbaric thing to say and it turned me on to feel so possessed in the moment. His cock slid deeper, each inch stretching me, until I felt full and his hips pressed against my ass.

"More," I mumbled when he slowly withdrew until he was nearly out of me.

Quinn pushed me forward onto my elbows and lifted my hips to give himself the angle he wanted. "Hold on, Katie, I'm going to fuck you now!"

Quinn's fingers dug into my flesh as he held my hips suspended above the bed, while he slammed into me from behind. I would be bruised from his grip, but I didn't care. I just wanted more.

"More," I said again. I couldn't get enough. I needed affirmation that Quinn was alive, and whole, and here with me.

My back arched as nerve endings I never knew existed screamed to life, and pleasure washed through me. Slow and deliberate strokes gave way to hard and fast thrusts, and it was oh-so-pleasurable when his heavy testicles spanked me as he slammed against my ass.

A heavy feeling began to grow in the pit of my stomach, and those unfinished waves of my first orgasm washed through me and began to build. We both made small grunting noises with the force of each stroke. I knew he was close when he lost his rhythm, but he wasn't finished with me yet.

Quinn slid a hand down my arm until he reached my hand. He threaded his fingers with mine and brought our clasped hands to his lips. The gentle kiss was a surprisingly sweet gesture. Then he moved us once again, placing our joined hands over my heart.

"Come for me, Katie, love," he whispered, his chest pressed tight against my back.

I clenched around his cock as his final pounding strokes took me screaming over the edge. He gave two short thrusts and then he was coming with me, spilling his hot seed inside me. He bit down on my neck as hard as the first time we'd made love. I screamed again and knew he'd marked me, but any pain was lost in the waves of pleasure that shot straight to my pussy.

When we collapsed, I thought we might sleep, but the insatiable Quinn had other ideas. He ran his hand lightly over my skin, caressing me from breasts to knees, and asked, "Are you okay, Katie?"

The gesture sent shudders through me, but before I could think why, Quinn scooped me up and carried me to the bathroom. After carefully adjusting the water, he set me inside and then joined me.

We stood together in the shower while I ran my hands over the unblemished skin of his chest. I'd seen the wounds last night. He *had* been shot. Had it really been Owen who had healed Quinn? Did I have something to do with it, as Quinn hinted last night? I realized that at this moment, I didn't care. I was just grateful he was alive and unhurt.

Quinn was too tall for us to fit well standing up, but when he lifted me and I wrapped my legs around his waist, we fit just right. He slid into me, hard, fast, deep. The water cascaded around us, a warm caress that made his golden skin sparkle. He filled me and then pulled out slowly, before thrusting home again. Each stroke was a slippery slice of heaven.

Quinn's hand dropped between my thighs and found my clit. And with a few strokes of his thumb and thrusts of his cock we orgasmed again, crashing together, shuddering hard beneath the warm spray.

Finally sated, for a while at least, Quinn once again carried me back to the bed and lay down naked beside me, our bodies still damp from the shower. He lay on his back, eyes closed, and soon his breathing became deep and steady. I snuggled against his side, my face nestled between his shoulder and his neck, and he held me close while he slept.

We still hadn't talked beyond the murmurs of sex. We hadn't discussed what happened last night. I still didn't know what Quinn was, although I was beginning to have some idea. I finally realized why Owen's gesture of running his hand over Quinn's body looked familiar. I'd seen Quinn himself do it first, the night he first made love to me. He'd not been gentle that night either, and I should have been sore. Instead, Quinn had brushed a hand over my skin, and all of my discomfort had eased. Owen was one of the Fae. A fairy. Did that mean—

I pushed the thought aside. It wasn't worth worrying about right now. So *what* if I didn't know what Quinn was? I didn't know what *I* was, either. I didn't know what the House wanted from me or what Joanne expected to happen when she'd arranged for me to come here after her death.

Juniper Springs might pretend to be Sedona's little cousin in all things metaphysical, but I knew that the truly unbelievable lived here. The location of the House couldn't be a coincidence. What was it about this particular part of the world that drew so many mythical creatures? And how was it that the sheriff knows them all? *Protects them all?*

This small community was the stuff of fairy tales, nightmares, and bad Hollywood movies. Werewolves, witches, and Fae...oh my! There was something here...something that tied all of the secrets together.

In spite of so many unknowns or perhaps because of them, I needed to remember what I had learned since coming to Juniper Springs. The Honey House might be a first class bed and breakfast, but it also was the first real home I'd ever known. A home—me? Who'd have thunk it?

With a small smile, I ran through the names: Gregory, Owen, Raymond, and Gabrielle. I suppose I needed to include Stevie now, though I'd only met him as a wolf.

These were all my people, maybe even something like a family.

Did Quinn belong with the others? Or was what I felt for him something more? When I'd thought he was dying, a terrified part of me feared he would be lost to me forever. Did that mean I—

Steel bands tightened around my chest, and Quinn pulled me over to lie on top of his chest.

"Mmm...Katie, love," he murmured against the marks on my neck. "You're thinking too damned hard. I have a much better use for all that excess energy," he said, as his hands smoothed down my back.

A delicious shiver shuddered through me as my mouth sought his. Yes, I wanted this...I wanted him. Quinn and I might not be the sort of people who believed in happily ever after, but maybe...just maybe, we could have a happily for now.

~~The End~~

About the Author

Raised in California, Laura likes it hot, which explains why she ended up in Arizona via such diverse places as Japan, Maine, and Florida, and many more places in between. After retiring from the US Navy, she found a niche working for land management agencies, including the National Park Service and the Bureau of Land Management. Though she has held many jobs around the world, her favorite was working and living in Grand Canyon National Park. Working (and eating) in New Orleans was a close second. You will find many of her books are set against the rich backdrops provided by coastal Louisiana and northern Arizona.

When asked how she started writing, Laura tells of waking on Boxing Day a few years ago, with a woman named Elena MacFarland yammering in her dreams, demanding her story be told. Despite never attempting to write fiction before that morning, Laura ignored all of the holiday visitors and the Highland Destiny series was born. She doesn't believe it was a coincidence that the great grandmother who died when Laura was just a baby was named Elena MacFarland. Destiny does play a hand.

Laura became a full-time writer in 2012, and now she spends her time writing, watching her Arizona Diamondbacks, and working on her very own version of the Willow Springs Ranch in northwestern Arizona. She is a multi-published author of erotic romance, mystery, and urban fantasy and her books can be found at all major online retailers.

Connect with Laura at:

Twitter: @LauraHarner

Facebook: facebook.com/lauraharner

Or even better…check out the website at: LauraHarner.com

Also Available

Forbidden Love

Detective Danielle Delacroiux is one kick-ass detective with the Généreux PD, and she's got a murder on her hands. By all accounts, Crease Martin was nothing but a homeless drunk and a lousy informant, but Dani counted him as one of hers. Now she'll stop at nothing to find his murderer. With a red silk handkerchief under the body as her first clue, Dani wants a quick break. When a handsome stranger practically strolls up to the crime scene, Dani can't help but notice his expensive Italian suit, red silk tie, and empty breast pocket. Could he be who she's looking for?

Dani is less than impressed when Mr. tall, dark, and yummy is introduced as the newest lawyer in town, and even worse, he's another of the Charbonnet offspring. The deadly feud between the Delacroiux and Charbonnet families goes way back, and there is one thing she knows without a doubt. If Hawk Charbonnet committed this crime, she'll be damned if his connections will do him any good. She'll happily lock his arrogant ass in jail for the rest of his life. Which would be a shame, because she had to admit, it was a fine-looking ass.

~*~

Altered States, free prologue for the Altered States Series

New Orleans Police Detective Sam Garrett can't believe his bad luck when he's assigned to investigate a string of gay-bashings turned deadly in the French Quarter. Especially when he realizes Travis Boudreaux, his new, hot, and most-likely-straight partner, plans to use him as bait. The worst part? They've got no back-up because the rest of the city is preoccupied by another series of killings — the victims drained of blood.

~*~

Deep Blues Goodbye, Book One of the Altered States Series

The world might not have been ready for vampires when NOPD Detective Travis Boudreaux had the bad taste to sit up at his own funeral, but two years later, the new cause célèbre is civil rights for preternatural beings and most humans are on the bandwagon. Except whoever is killing vampires and wannabes.

Detective Sam Garrett hates all things preternatural. Having your undead partner try to make you his first meal will do that to a guy. One final screw-up gets Sam banished to the Paranormal Criminal Investigations Unit—the Odd Squad—under the oversight of Detective Danny Burkette.

Now it's up to Burkette to work with Garrett by day and Boudreaux by night as they follow a trail of clues that leads from the historic cemeteries of New Orleans to the bayous of southern Louisiana. Under the all-too-interested gaze of a Master vampire and the local werewolf pack Alpha, they discover some lessons in life—and death—take longer to learn...and not all second chances are created equal.

Warning: In this series the vampires don't sparkle, werewolves kill, and sometimes the men have sex. With each other.

~*~

Ty Hard, Book One of the Willow Springs Ranch Series

Tyler has used Don't Ask, Don't Tell as a shield against the truth since he was seventeen. Now, Ty finds himself cut loose from his Navy career after months of rehab from a debilitating head injury. At a loss as to what to do with his life, he travels to Willow Springs Ranch in Arizona to visit his surrogate father, only to arrive minutes after his oldest friend's death. Ty must come to terms with the loss while he fights to keep the PTSD from pulling him under. The last thing he's ready to think about is his growing attraction for another man.

Rancher Cass Cartwright's relationships never last more than a few hours, and that's just the way he likes it.

Now he's in danger of doing the one thing he swore never to do: fall in love. Can Cass convince Ty to let go of his past or will sabotage at the ranch kill their love before it has a chance to grow?

~*~

Hold Tight, Book Two of the Willow Spring Ranch Series

Sheriff Holden Titus had organized his fresh start down to the last detail. Except for the part about the bomb that blew his plans all to hell. Now he's running out of time, without a job, without a home, and struggling to get back on his feet. Literally.

Despite the impolite rejection, Drew knows he didn't have the wrong impression months ago when he asked the sheriff to dance, but he never expected to have Holden's life in his hands. Literally.

Thanks to some meddlesome matchmaking, the two men are now temporary housemates at the Willow Springs Ranch and Drew is determined to help Holden heal, both physically and emotionally. Even if it means he has to drag the other man kicking and screaming to physical therapy…and out of the closet. In fact, that might be kind of fun.

The problem is, Holden doesn't consider himself in the closet…but not all secrets are created equal.

~*~

Rescued, Book, Two of the Three's Allowed Series

Elizabeth Ashford runs into the wilderness near a highway rest area, trying to escape her abusive husband before he kills her. Self-made millionaire and expert in high tech security, Michael Enwright is at the first rest stop of his long overdue sabbatical when he sees the fleeing woman and intervenes, saving Elizabeth's life, while nearly losing his own. When Michael's help is misinterpreted, he ends up handcuffed and face down in the dirt before Elizabeth can set her former lover, Sheriff Graeme Kennedy, straight. In order to protect Lizzie, Graeme is forced to work with Michael and brings both of them to his cabin for protection.

Now Graeme finally has Elizabeth under his roof, right where he's always wanted her. So why is he jacking off to visions of the drop dead gorgeous and take-charge Michael? Some things never change.